USA Book News "Best Books of 2011" Finalist

Gold Medal Award – Readers' Favorite 2010

"An absorbing read . . . Josiah Reynolds is a unlikely and compelling new crime solver." Neil Chethik, author of FatherLoss and VoiceMale

"Abigail Keam's riveting mystery debut features a superb sleuth, Josiah Reynolds, whose wit and grit are perfectly suited to the wily turns of the plot. Bluegrass readers will rejoice at a fine, new voice from our region and others will be delighted by the mix of art, rural beauty, and intrigue. Suspenseful, funny and imaginative, *Death By A HoneyBee* is a fantastic read." Lynn Pruett, author of Ruby River

"We are introduced to a cast of characters and a storyline that, like honey, is sweet and delicious." Linda Hinchcliff, Chevy Chase Magazine

"I do wish you every success with your endeavor and I trust that you're hard at work on the next." Sue Grafton, author of Kinsey Millhone series, U

"*Death By A HoneyBee* is an enjoyable read which will capture the interest of the most die-hard mystery readers." Reader's Favorite

Death By A HoneyBee

Death By A HoneyBee
A Josiah Reynolds Mystery

Abigail Keam

Worker Bee Press

ISBN 978-0-61534734-9

Published in the USA by

Worker Bee Press
P.O. Box 485
Nicholasville, KY 40340

Abigail Keam

The author wishes to thank
Deborah Struve and Phil Criswell
Who took the time to read the
unrevised ms and offered comments.

Thanks to Rebecca Webster
and Diana Keam for their encouragement.

Thanks to William O'Connor MD, Professor of Pathology and
Laboratory Medicine, UK College of Medicine, for letting me pick
his brain at a dinner party.
Thanks to Gerald Marvel, General Manager of Spindletop Hall
Inc., who gave me detailed information
and even made corrections on the Spindletop chapter for me.
www.spindletophall.org.
Thanks to glass artist Stephen Powell who consented to be a
character, www.powellglass.com, and
Al's Bar which consented to be used as a drinking hole
for my poetry-writing cop, Kelly.

And thanks to the Lexington Farmers' Market,
which has given me a home for many years.
www.lexingtonfarmersmarket.com

Very special thanks to my mother, Mabel Louise,
for passing on her love of movies and reading to me.

Special thanks to Neil Chethik, best selling author, and
Author in Residence at the Carnegie Center for Literacy,
who kept pushing me forward. www.neilchethik.com

And to my editor, Brian Throckmorton,
for his corrections and insight into the characters.

For Peter,
Who makes my life possible.

Abigail Keam

1

I knew something was wrong as I turned the corner around the copse of black walnut trees where mourning doves roosted. The stillness of the gray-breasted birds perched in a dull slash on a tree limb contrasted with the clamorous buzzing of thousands of bees. As though readying for battle, their thundering racket was an alarm that meant danger to anyone or anything that chanced upon them in their harried state.

As a mother knows the meaning of her baby's whimpering, so a beekeeper understands the droning of her bees. I thought an animal might have disturbed them – a raccoon, or maybe a deer, had kicked over a hive. That alone would cause them to be anxious and making it difficult for me to work with them. I hurried past the vigilant doves, their heads swiveling in my direction. Coming around a hedge of honeysuckle, I encountered a six-foot-high wall of enraged bees hovering between their white hives and me, a glittering wave of golden insects ready to inflict painful stings on anything deemed hostile.

Thank goodness I had worn my thick white cotton beesuit as honeybees hurled themselves at my veil in a panic. To be accosted this aggressively is unnerving even for the most experienced beekeeper. I felt my stomach muscles tighten. Talk about a gut feeling.

"Babies, babies," I cooed. "Settle down. Settle down." Then I saw the source of their fear and revulsion. The metal cover from the most populous beehive had been heedlessly thrown on the ground, and wooden rectangle frames full of baby brood lay abandoned next to it. Thousands of young nurse bees frantically tried to protect this nursery full of eggs and wax-capped unborn bees by covering the frames with their bodies. This violation alone would make honeybees angry, but I saw that someone was bent over and plunged face down into the open hive, which made them even wilder. The person's arms hung down outside the hive. I noticed the fists were clenched.

"What are you doing?" I yelled, startled at the sight of a strange person with his head and shoulders inside one of my hives. "Who are you? Get away from there!" I stepped back waiting for a response.

My chest tightened. Hoping to stave off an asthma attack, I reached in my pocket for my abuterol spray, but realized my veil would stop me from getting the medicine to my mouth. I breathed more slowly. I inhaled the musky odor of the bees along with the heavy, cloying scent of honeysuckle hedges behind their hives. Somewhere in the distance I heard the growl of a tractor cutting sweet hay. I flinched at the sudden piercing call of a redwing blackbird.

I scanned the field for further danger. Other than a person sticking his naked head into one of my hives with eighty thousand bees dive-bombing him and me, nothing appeared different. The rest of the hives waited in line like sailors standing at attention in their white uniforms. Bullets of reflected light darted back and forth from openings in the bottom hive boxes so quickly the human eye could barely register the tiny insects. Freshly mowed grass manicured the ground around the hives. Their water tank, full of hyacinths and duckweed, stood unmolested.

The intruder did not stir. Grasping a fallen branch from the ground along with my belching hive smoker thrust before me, I moved closer. "Mister," I cried, "MISTER!" I assumed it was a he – a heavy-set man with pale skin – in beige corduroy pants and laced-up boots. I called again. Still, he did not budge.

My initial shock overcome, I realized he didn't seem to be breathing. *Not a good sign.* The bees covered him, pulling and biting at his neck, stinging his scalp and his back, furiously trying to evict him from their home. I inched closer. He looked stiff. I poked him with my branch. He didn't shift. I jabbed him again with the tree branch. Nothing.

Leaning over the body, I carefully swatted away the bees. "Girls, girls, don't sting him. It's over. Don't waste yourselves," I whispered. Still the bees stung him and, by doing so, condemned themselves to death too. The man's neck swelled against his checkered shirt. I took off my glove to feel for a pulse but the bees swamped my hand, stinging furiously. I pulled away quickly. "Merde!" I exclaimed. I cradled my badly stung hand.

I walked away from the hives, yanking off my beekeeper's hat and veil. I fumbled in my suit for my cell phone. My hands were shaking as I dialed 911. "Police? You better come. I have a dead man in my beehive. Yes, that is correct.

He is lying face down in a beehive." I gave the police my
name and address, clicked the phone shut and sat on the
meadow grass waiting for the wail of the police siren.
It seemed like a long time before they came.

2

My name is Josiah Reynolds. My maternal grandmother, who felt compelled to give biblical masculine names to the girls in her family, gave name to me. She said it was to make us strong. My mother's name was Micah. People always mistook her name for mica, a silicate mineral. However, I love my moniker, being named after a king.

For the past three years, I have made my living from working the land – mainly beekeeping. My home is built on a cliff overlooking the forest-green, fast-flowing Kentucky River. Following the river east of my farm, Daniel Boone built Fort Boonesborough. North is Ashland, former estate of Henry Clay, the Great Compromiser and statesman who owned slaves; south lies White Hall, the haunted home to Cassius Clay, a distant cousin of Henry's who was a firebrand emancipationist. Legend has it that the moment Cassius Clay breathed his last, lightning struck Henry Clay's towering memorial statue in the Lexington Cemetery, decapitating it.

The blue and grey once skirmished on my property. I still find Civil War uniform buttons, as well as arrowheads from the Shawnees who used to hunt here. I suspect that a small hill on my land might be a Native American Adena burial mound. I stay away from it out of respect, and I will not let the Anthropology Department at the University of Kentucky excavate it.

I think it was Faulkner who said, "The past is never dead. It is not even past." My neighbors would concur, and so do I. Like a blue morning mist hovering over the Kentucky River, the history of this land hangs tight. The past is always tapping on my shoulder. It never strays far from anyone who lives in Caintuck, the dark and bloody ground, as I would find out later. It was going to bite me but good, but I didn't realize this when I found the body. Looking back, I was naive, plain and simple. Like most women, I didn't sense the danger coming my way.

I am a beekeeper, and a good one at that. Since most of my current income derives from selling honey at the local Farmers' Market, I am always concerned about my bees. As a rule, they receive better medical attention and general care than I do. So I was pretty agitated when I saw police officers poking around my hives even to the point of banging on their sides. Of course, the guard bees of these hives responded by swarming the offenders. A cop angrily pulled a fire extinguisher out of his cruiser trunk after being stung several times.

"Don't you dare use that on my bees!" I yelled. I glared at the coroner struggling into his hazmat suit.

"Yes, put that away or you'll contaminate the scene," the coroner said, putting on his headgear after crushing a cigarette in the grass. He and two other officers looked like Michelin

Men as they waddled through quick darts of bees. Most of the field bees had already headed out to harvest nectar from wildflowers in the surrounding pastures. Their daily routine was not going to be hampered by a dead body in their neighbors' hive. Field bees, already returning from pastures laden with flower juice, expertly swerved around men standing in their pathways. Both smell and sight guided them home among a row of twenty painted white hives. Honeybees can fly forward, backwards or sideways at fifteen miles per hour, so they are able to swerve around strange obstacles in their way.

"Quit swatting at those bees," I cried. "It only makes them mad."

"This is rich," said a voice at my elbow. I looked up to see my helper, Matt, standing beside me suited up, but with his veil off.

I smiled inside. Matt was six feet two with dark curly hair and blue eyes. He looked like Victor Mature, the matinee idol of the 40's and 50's. I thought Victor Mature was the most delicious male I had ever beheld after seeing him in *The Robe*. And he even had a sense of humor. When an exclusive country club refused Mature membership because he was an actor, the Louisville homeboy protested, "I am not an actor. Haven't you seen my movies?" Good looking and funny. What woman could resist that combination?

Many thought Matt and I were lovers, which was ridiculous. Why would this Adonis be bedding a frumpy middle-aged woman? But the rumors did give me a source of pride. So I never told my straight friends that he was gay. And neither did he. He was that good of a friend to support my vanity.

"Who is it?" Matt asked, seemingly unperturbed at the commotion in the beeyard. He acted more intrigued than worried, but then it wasn't really his problem.

"No idea," I shrugged.

The state's bee inspector, Caleb Noble, pulled up in his jeep, flashed the cops his badge and began recording the proceedings.

"Hell's bells," I murmured to Matt. "Somebody called Caleb. Like I don't have enough trouble."

The coroner and two assistants measured and probed the body with forbidding-looking instruments. They filled evidence bags, sealed them and made notes on a log. The police photographer took pictures. Satisfied, the coroner gave the word for his guys to yank the body out of the hive. Honeybees fell lifelessly from the victim's hair. One coroner's assistant put some dead bees in a jar for testing. The victim's face was gooey with streaks of honey and mashed bee pollen. Great clumps of beeswax fell from his swollen jowls to the ground. An acrid smell drifted from the disturbed hive.

Matt groaned, "Oh man. That is nasty looking." I was glad to see Matt finally unnerved.

The victim's face was not recognizable due to the lumpy swelling from hundreds of bee stings. It looked like a huge red beet, the kind that wins prizes at fairs.

"I don't know how this could have happened," I said. "What was he doing here?"

"Are you sure it is a he? Who could tell from that thing?" Matt looked away from the awful sight.

I concurred that it was a hard spectacle to behold.

"You know that they will probably take that hive as evidence, or at least some of the frames," said Matt.

I sighed. "You'd better put another hive box together. Take some frames with honey from the other hives. Some brood, too, if they can spare it. Just save what you can. I hope they don't kill the Queen with their meddlin'."

Matt pulled out his cell phone and started taking pictures.

I stared at him in silent annoyance.

"If Caleb is video-recording, then I should take pictures," he argued, scanning the scene with his phone. "Here he comes."

I looked over. He was also carrying samples of dead bees.

"Yes, we better take pictures. Just in case," repeated Matt.

"In case of what?"

"You know – in case you get sued."

"Sued for what? I should sue that person's family for destruction of my property."

Matt assumed his superior lawyer's look. "It has been my limited experience that usually it is the property owner that gets the crap stomped out of him, in this case her, both in and out of court."

"As if you have even tried your first case," I snorted. I looked at the body now being zipped into a black bag with plastic handles. "I think that poor schmuck is the one who got stomped on."

"Morning, Miss Josiah. Got quite a mess here," said Caleb, making notes as he approached me. He was dressed in white coveralls and had his bee hat tied around his waist. "Know what happened?"

I took my time replying. Whatever I said was going into an official report to Frankfort, and Caleb had the power to make my life miserable. "That guy was probably drunk or high and got the bright idea of stealing some hives."

"Any possibility that these bees are Africanized and attacked without provocation?"

16

"You can test them if you like but . . ." I held out my hand where several bees settled. I poked them. The bees merely scraped pollen into the pollen basket on their hind legs and flew off. "They don't seem too aggressive to me. I think these are all European bees." It was every beekeeper's nightmare that their pure European stock would become compromised with African DNA, making the bees a hundred times more aggressive. Instead of being stung ten times by honeybees, a person would be stung a hundred times and be chased for one thousand feet or more. The problem was that Africanized bees looked just like European bees. To protect myself against possible aggression, I always wore my suit into the beeyard until I could establish that the bees were friendly. If they were, I usually stripped down to a pair of pants, long sleeved shirt and a veil. Other times they were cranky and I kept the suit on.

Caleb wiped the sweat from his forehead. "They look pretty gentle to me too, but I am going to check their DNA anyway."

"Fine with me," I said. "I'll let you go about your business then."

"Will call you if I find anything odd."

"Sounds good, Caleb." I watched the inspector move towards my hives.

"Where is his car, Rennie?" Matt used his pet name for me because I could recite Michael Rennie's lines to the robot in *The Day the Earth Stood Still.* We share a love of old movies. It was how we met.

Three years ago, I was a guest at a Kentucky Derby party when I heard Matt arguing with another man about the commands to the robot. Apparently they had a bet on it.

"Klaatu barada nikto," I whispered into Matt's ear. "The

robot's name was Gort and the actress was Patricia Neal."

Matt turned around with surprised eyes and said, "Well hello, Gorgeous!"

"Barbra Streisand as Fannie Brice in *Funny Girl*," I replied.

"Marry me," Matt quipped as he collected his money. After talking into the wee hours of the night, it seemed that we both were batty about movies. In fact, he came with me to watch *Double Indemnity* that night only to fall asleep in my car on the way home. I awoke the next morning to find Matt leaning on my car drinking coffee while watching a flock of wild turkeys skirt around the house. He really hadn't left my side since then. I believed his devotion has been due to my collection of four hundred and seventy-two videos and DVDs. We watched a movie every week. It was a standing date.

Pushing those fond memories away, I responded to Matt's assessment of the current situation. "Oh," I said, scanning the fields. Great response, huh.

"Something for you to study on," Matt said, firmly snapping away. "The question of this poor slob's transportation."

I snorted – but then again, Matt had recently passed his bar exam and now worked at a prestigious corporate law firm. He helped me only during his days off, calling beekeeping his therapy from the overachievers, backstabbers and just plain scum. He was referring to his colleagues – not his clients.

"Sure. Go ahead and take all the pictures you want. I am going back to the house. I have a whale of a headache," I said while watching the police put yellow caution tape around my hives.

"Take a breathing treatment," he called after me. "You're wheezing."

I put my hand on my chest. Indeed I was.

18

3

A sharp knock woke me from a dream of my late husband. It was just as well. I surely didn't want to waste my time with him now that he's dead. I got up from my comfortable retro couch, groggy from a late afternoon nap. My medicine sometimes made me sleepy.

"Just a moment," I called as I ambled to the steel front double door straightening my shirt. I led a plain-clothes policeman through the welcoming shade of my bamboo and water alcove, and into the great room with its walls of gray concrete and bold abstract paintings of jarring color.

"I am Detective O'nan. I'm primary on this investigation. We're finished for now," O'nan said, scanning the room and my things. He showed me his police ID. His first name was Fred. I was surprised I didn't see a badge like cops flash on TV. "I just need to take a preliminary statement. We can take a more formal statement later if something turns up."

"Turns up?"

"Just routine," Detective O'nan assured, taking out a notebook. "In case you remember something else. I already talked with your assistant, Matt," he said looking at his notes.

O'nan looked to be in his late thirties. He was wearing an expensive dark suit that emphasized his powerful, wide shoulders and narrow waist. His stylish haircut played down his thinning blond hair. I noticed his nails were professionally manicured. He reminded me of Tab Hunter. Standing ramrod straight, O'nan towered over me. His metallic blue eyes never seemed to leave my face. They betrayed a hardness that I suspected didn't have anything to do with working homicide cases.

"I got up, dressed, went to work in the beeyard and found . . . what you saw. I called – you came. End of story." I gaped curiously at O'nan. His youthful face seemed familiar to me, but I couldn't place him.

"Unhuh," he said, taking notes. "Anything unusual happen that you noticed before you found the body – sounds? Anything?"

"Nothing." I shook my head. "It has been quite a shock."

"I'm sure." His eyes narrowed.

I stared at the floor. Finally, I said, "There is nothing else to tell."

"Okay." He flipped out a business card and handed it to me. As O'nan turned to go, he saw Matt walk through the door. "If you think of anything, give me a call."

I glanced at the card. "All right." Thinking of my bees, I asked, "Hey, can I get back in the beeyard? My bees need to be watered and powdered," referring to the technique of dusting them with powdered sugar. By grooming, they knock off parasites. It was a holistic way of treating for mites.

"Yes, we are completely finished. The crime tape is still up but you can go underneath it."

"That's good."

Matt strode past me into the kitchen, pulled the refrigerator door open, and drank out of a milk carton.

O'nan gave him a quick once-over. I don't think he liked what he saw. His left cheek quivered for just a moment before he glanced back at me.

"I can see myself out." He turned and was gone.

I faced Matt. "He thinks you're my fancy man."

"How about taking your fancy man out to a late lunch? I just can't do any work with this happening. Bad juju. Besides, the bees need to calm down before I go back out."

"Uptown or downtown?"

"Ramsey's is fine."

"How is my hair?"

Matt gave me a lascivious look. "You always look sexy."

I grinned and snapped my fingers. "That is why you will always have a place at my table," I replied. I swept through the door he had opened for me.

He chuckled when he saw a tangled knot of hair protruding from the back of my head. Matt loved playing pranks on me. As much as Matt played to my vanity, he also treasured knocking it down. He had a touch of sadist in him and only told me about the knot after twenty people had seen it and I wondered aloud why people were staring at me. It was just enough tension to keep me from falling in love with Matt. Maybe that is why he did it. He liked our relationship just the way it was. Rumors about us were one thing. Reality was another.

4

I was getting dressed for the Farmers' Market a week later when I received a telephone call from Detective O'nan. Would I be so kind as to stop by the police station after the Market? They just had a few more questions to tie up before they closed the case. Sure – why not. I never suspected a thing, when a little bell should have been ringing in my head.

The station is only blocks from the Market so I left my rusty but durable VW van at my booth location, with a note on the van's windshield that I would be returning by four p.m. Each vendor has his/her own 10x10 spot where they park under a tree-lined canopy and sell to the public. There were still some farmers conducting business. During the summer peak, there could be as many as seventy farmers working the Market, which was considered one of the finest in the country. The sales paid my basic bills plus food, and I enjoyed serving my loyal customers who were always pleased to see me. It made me feel needed.

I swept back my red hair while asking for Detective O'nan at the front desk of the police station, housed in a renovated department store. I lifted my work apron to wipe the grime off my face.

Minutes later, Detective O'nan and an overweight man with hairy arms stepped into the waiting room.

I shuddered. I always dislike the look of men who appear part simian. It was a big turnoff for me. Then I felt ashamed of my hypocrisy, as I could probably braid the hair on my legs. Thank goodness I had worn pants.

Both men shook my hand before asking me to accompany them. That warning bell should have gone off then, but it didn't. They ushered me into a dull gray room with one table and four chairs. There was no window but a mirror that I suspected was a two-way. The room smelled of Lysol sprayed over the odor of perspiration created by fear. Cigarette burns patterned the desk beside carved obscene words. There were several swastikas tattooed in ink. *Lovely.* I was afraid to look underneath to see the collection of old gum and crusts of bodily fluids deposited there. Two chairs repaired with duct tape waited at the table. Even though my knees were burning from arthritis, I stood after O'nan motioned me to sit in a chair.

"Can't you take a statement at your desk?" I asked, scrutinizing the dismal area. "This looks like an interrogation room." I chuckled at the suggestion, trying to lighten the mood, but both cops remained stone-faced.

"Something rather unusual has come up, Josiah," said Detective O'nan. He sat down and tossed several files on the table. "This will give us some privacy to get to the bottom."

"The bottom of what, Fred?"

"Detective O'nan," he corrected.

"Okay, then it is Mrs. Reynolds," I shot back.

He frowned. I could tell he was a man who didn't like to be corrected.

The hairy fat man leaned forward. "You're not from around here? Your accent."

"And you are again?" I finally sat as my legs were giving out.

He smiled, a lovely smile with dimples. "I'm sorry. I am Detective Goetz. I noticed that your accent is Midwestern. I just wondered."

"I am from northern Kentucky."

"Where about?"

"Boone and Kenton counties."

"That explains it." Goetz smiled again and sat on the corner of the table. "Do you still say 'please' for 'excuse me?' Dead giveaway for someone from up around the Cincinnati area."

"Yes, I still do. Are you from up there?"

"Went to Holmes High School."

"No kidding. I used to date a boy from Holmes."

"Josiah is an unusual name for a woman," Goetz commented.

"My grandmother thought if it was good enough for a Judean king, it was good enough for me."

"As I remember, Josiah was a righteous king who destroyed prostitution in the Temple."

"Male prostitution, actually."

"Really?"

"And you do what now?" interjected O'nan. *He must be the "bad" cop in this scenario,* I thought.

"I'm a beekeeper."

Goetz shifted in his seat. "Really, that must be interesting. Where do you sell your honey?"

"At the Farmers' Market a couple days a week. I have a small apiary."

Abigail Keam

"Any other beekeepers in the market?" asked O'nan.

"Yes. There is a Mrs. Simons who specializes in honey body care products and a Rick Niles who sells varietal honey, but he also does beeswax items like candles. I only sell honey."

Goetz shot O'nan a look. "Anyone else?"

I coughed. "No one that I would like to discuss." I felt my chest begin to tighten.

"Isn't there another beekeeper who is a member of the Market?"

Before I could answer, O'nan cleared his throat. "Mrs. Reynolds, do you know the victim?"

"Not that I am aware of."

"Are you sure?"

"I didn't recognize the clothing except that it looked masculine. I'm sure that it was a man – right?"

O'nan nodded.

"None of my neighbors have turned up missing so I don't know this man." I looked at both of them. "I swear I didn't recognize the man. Aren't you going to tell me who he is . . . or was?"

"Do you know a Richard Pidgeon?" asked O'nan while writing in his notebook.

I slumped back into the chair, clamping my lips together.

The detectives exchanged glances.

"Yes, I know him. What has he got to do with this?"

"Isn't he a member of the Market?" inquired Goetz.

"Yes," I said grudgingly.

"He is the man stung to death by your bees."

I surveyed the depressing gray walls in order to avoid eye contact with them. "I think I'd better call a lawyer."

The deep lines in Detective Goetz's face sagged. "Perhaps you had better."

I pulled my cell phone out of my work apron and dialed. Matt answered on the second ring. "Matt, get me a good criminal lawyer quick or else get your ass over here to the police station pronto. It was Richard Pidgeon dead in my hive." I snapped the phone shut. Closing my eyes, I announced, "I haven't anything else to say until my lawyer gets here." The detectives snatched up their files and exited, leaving me alone in the dingy room.

I knew I was in trouble. That little bell, which should have gone off earlier, was now clanging loud and clear.

5

Matt strode into the interrogation room an hour and ten minutes later accompanied by a black woman with a platinum blonde crew cut. The woman never looked at me, but placed her Vuitton leather briefcase on the battered, nicked wooden desk.

"Anything you want to tell me?" she said with a faint British clip as she fiddled with her beige silk jacket, still not looking at me.

Matt discreetly motioned to me to be cooperative. "I don't know how that man got there. I had nothing to do with it." I stole a confused look at Matt.

"What have you told the police?" she inquired, finally training her eyes on me. They burned with an intensity that I have witnessed only in saints, great artists and a few of the homeless wandering around downtown in Phoenix Park.

"Nothing. As soon as they told me it was Richard Pidgeon, I called Matt. I didn't say another word."

"Have you touched anything like a glass or mug? Have you asked for anything to drink?"

"Noooooo."

"Good. Then they don't have anything with your fingerprints on it." Still, she didn't look convinced. "Matt has filled me in on the particulars. We need to find out what they want with you, but I really don't advise my clients to talk to the police. You should never have set foot in the police station. Have you ever heard of Richard Jewell?"

"No," I replied.

"He found a bomb at the 1996 Summer Olympics in Atlanta, saving many lives. You know how he was repaid? The law tried to set him up as the bomber, using his cooperation in the case as evidence against him. Jewell's life was ruined until he started fighting back with lawsuits. Eventually another man, Eric Robert Rudolph, confessed.

"You never cooperate with the police, Mrs. Reynolds. JonBenet Ramsey's family knew that. Same thing. A case was built against them while the media tried them in public. Years later it was released that the DNA evidence was not from any of the family members, but that was little comfort to the family. By then, Mrs. Ramsey was dead."

"I just want to clear this matter up," I replied. "I've got nothing to hide."

"It seems like plain vandalism gone bad to me." The criminal lawyer swung her hazel eyes towards Matt.

Matt held up his hands in defeat. "Don't confer with me. I just passed my bar exam six months ago. I don't know what they want of Mrs. Reynolds."

"I would think that if anything occurred it would be a civil lawsuit from the man's family asking for damages." She paused, lost in thought. "It seems odd to me that they have you in an interrogation room." She leaned to scratch her leg framed in expensive but conservative black leather pumps.

With that platinum hair, why bother trying to be conservative, I thought.

"My problem is your daughter wants to know what this is about, and I am to call her in an hour. Let's see what they want but don't answer anything until I nod. Okay?" Leaning over me, she said in a very low voice. "I'm doing this as a favor for your daughter. You jack me around, you'll wish you hadn't."

I swung around glaring accusingly at Matt.

"I had to call. She knows the lawyer to get for this. For God's sakes, I'm a tax lawyer, babe," Matt replied, loosening his tie.

"Are you the best?" I asked the woman.

"You bet."

"Then I can't afford you."

She glared at me as if I had just piddled on her expensive shoes. "I thought I had made myself clear. Your daughter has made certain arrangements with me. As your daughter is a silent partner of your farm, she is entitled to have anything concerning the farm legally represented by me."

"What total bull!" I sputtered.

She capped her Mont Blanc pen. "What's it going to be? We can see what they want, only if you listen to me before answering. Or we can walk."

"Matt?" I pleaded.

He shook his head. "Josiah, I don't know what to tell you. Sometimes if you don't talk to them, it makes the police think you have something to hide. And then, if you do talk to them, you can stumble and say something stupid that really puts them on your scent. It's fifty-fifty," countered Matt.

I realize that a death in my beeyard was not something from which I was going to walk away. I couldn't pretend it hadn't happened. I nodded slightly.

29

My newly appointed lawyer motioned to Matt. "Do tell those very nice policemen who are watching us behind the mirror to come into the room. We are ready to proceed – that is, if it is convenient for them." She pasted on a phony smile. I was surprised her teeth weren't pointed like a shark's.

*

O'nan switched on the video camera.

"How official is this?" asked my lawyer, whose name I learned was Shaneika Mary Todd.

"Let's just say we are concerned and have some questions. This is just an informal talk," O'nan replied.

"Yeah, right," muttered Matt.

"We are entitled to a copy of the tape you are making," Ms. Todd demanded.

"Oh sure," replied O'nan as he leaned forward, unbuttoning his jacket. I sensed he was lying.

Ms. Todd pulled a tape recorder from her briefcase. She pushed a button. "Just in case your video gets lost."

A faint smile appeared on Detective Goetz's face before vanishing like a magician's coin.

O'nan proceeded. "Your full name, please?" he asked pushing a microphone towards me.

"Josiah Louise Reynolds."

"Address?"

"Route 169, Lexington, Kentucky."

"Occupation?"

"Beekeeper."

O'nan looked over his notes at me. "You are a professor at the University of Kentucky."

"Yes, ummm no, both my husband and I were professors. I was a professor of art history, specializing in religious art. My husband was a professor of architecture. Brannon, my husband, also had his own architectural firm. He is deceased."

Ms. Todd broke in. "Just answer what they ask," she warned me.

I nodded. "I retired three years ago after his death."

Ms. Todd pressed me under the table.

"I am sorry," I said to no one in particular. "I guess I'm nervous."

"Why is my client here?" interrupted Ms. Todd. "Isn't this just a simple accident? A tragedy I'm sure, but my client is not responsible for some misbehavior on a vandal's part."

Detective O'nan leaned back in his chair. "Well, here's the problem. The coroner's preliminary report came back yesterday, and there are some unanswered questions. It seems that Mr. Pidgeon died from a heart attack."

"There you go," I blurted confidently.

"More tests are being done. But what we want to know is what was he doing on your property around your hives?"

I shrugged.

O'nan opened a manila folder taking out some official-looking documents. "It seems that you and Mr. Pidgeon knew each other."

"He was a fellow beekeeper," I replied coldly.

"He *was* a very strong competitor of yours. We have reports that you two disliked each other. It even got to the point that you and he would not speak to each other," stated O'nan.

I kept quiet as Shaneika pressed her hand against my thigh.

O'nan continued, "We find it curious that someone you disliked, even hated, would be on your property, messing with your hives without a protective suit on and end up dead."

My answer tumbled out. "He is a charmer."

"Please?" said Goetz.

"He is . . . was a bee charmer." I looked at their stunned faces. "Like a horse whisperer – you know – a bee charmer. He never wore suits or any protective clothing. He didn't need to. Bees never stung him."

"Your bees stung him 176 times. Don't you think that is odd, Mrs. Reynolds, a bee charmer who never got stung has a heart attack in your beeyard and is stung 176 times?"

"Excuse me, but has the body been transferred to the medical examiner's office in Frankfort?" asked Ms. Todd.

O'nan ignored her while keeping his menacing gaze fixed directly on me.

Goetz joined in. "Also, where was his car?"

"Don't know," I replied.

"How did he get there?"

"I . . . I don't know," I stammered, my voice high with strain.

O'nan fiddled in his jacket pocket as though searching for a pack of cigarettes and then, apparently remembering he had stopped smoking, returned his attention to me. "I have several witnesses who stated that the two of you had a very public argument at the Kentucky State Fair where you threatened him only a month ago."

Matt jumped in. "I was there and she did no such thing. *He* threatened *her!*"

O'nan shot a look of annoyance at Matt and then referred to his notes again. "Didn't you say that you would hurt him?"

"It was the other way around." My chest tightened. "He cheated. He switched his tags with my jars and won the blue ribbon."

"And this blue ribbon is of some importance?" asked O'nan.

"It is the holy grail of beekeeping," I replied.

"How did he have the correct claim tag numbers then?"

"I had left them in an open cardboard box on the judges' table while I arranged my jars in the cabinet. Later, he must have just switched the tags on the jars and substituted the claim numbers with mine from the box when no one was looking."

"Apparently, when you lost, you accused him but couldn't prove it. There was an argument and you pushed him," stated Goetz, lazily leaning against the wall.

"No, he pushed me. I just pushed back. It . . . was like a reflex, you know – instinctive."

"Wasn't it your fault that Pidgeon fell into a glass display case, shattering it?"

"I was only defending myself. He didn't bring charges because he pushed me first . . . and he didn't get hurt from the broken glass."

"Why didn't you press charges then, if he assaulted you first as you claim?"

"Because I felt like a fool . . . and I didn't want this incident to get into the papers."

"Would that have anything to do with your daughter?"

My back stiffened. "My daughter has nothing to do with this nor any knowledge of it," I lied.

"All right boys, where are you going with this?" interjected Ms. Todd. "So my client and Mr. Pidgeon didn't like each other. They loathed each other – so what? He wanted revenge so he came to sabotage Mrs. Reynolds' hives. All hopped up with excitement and glee, he has a heart attack and dies."

"That is one possible scenario. But there is still the puzzle of the missing vehicle," interrupted O'nan.

It was Goetz's turn. "You could have picked him up and brought him out to your place. That would explain why he had no car."

"Why would I do that?"

"Perhaps you called and said you wanted to make amends. Wanted to talk with him and then lured him out to the beeyard."

I stood up. "That is ridiculous. Why would I even contact him?"

O'nan looked at me evenly. "We have your cell phone records and his number is listed. You made a call to him three days before his death."

"That's a lie. I never called Richard Pidgeon. Ever!"

Goetz interjected, "Would you be willing to take a polygraph test?"

"Sure, anything to clear this up," I responded. My chest felt tight.

Ms. Todd put her hand on my arm and gently pulled me back into my seat as she leaned in toward the detectives. "Mrs. Reynolds will not be taking any lie-detector test, handwriting analysis or DNA test unless through a court order. You are not to interview my client without moi being present," she said pointing to herself. She turned to me. "Don't you see what they are doing? The police don't ask for lie detector tests in accidental deaths."

I felt like an animal helplessly caught in a trap. My breathing became heavier.

Matt handed me an extra asthma inhaler he always carried around with him.

"Are you . . . are you suggesting murder?" I sputtered. To even say the word tasted bitter.

"Do you have any proof that my client killed Mr. Pidgeon . . . or even that this is a murder?" questioned Ms. Todd.

"I never uttered the word murder." O'nan turned to Goetz. "Did you ever say this was a murder?"

"Nope. Just a friendly inquiry."

Ms. Todd threw her legal pad into her briefcase and slapped it shut. "You guys are just on a fishing trip. Either tell us something concrete or we're walking." She stared at them.

They both returned her scathing look but were mum.

"Just as I thought," she retorted. She abruptly stood, grabbing her briefcase and me, propelling us both towards the door. "Gentlemen, we are done here."

Matt trotted after us along the scuffed yellow floor line pointing the way out of the building. It wasn't until we were several blocks away from the police station that Ms. Todd turned her fury upon me. "You are not to have any contact with anyone in law enforcement. I mean it. You should have told me that you came to blows with Richard Pidgeon! I went in there blind. Didn't I tell you not to play me?"

I wasn't brought up with such a jaded attitude. Innocent people were . . . well, innocent. I wasn't thinking clearly, but I did hear Ms. Todd say to Matt, "Take her home and make sure that she doesn't talk to them again without me. I will make some calls. See what's going on."

And with that, Shaneika Mary Todd was gone.

Matt returned me to my booth space only to discover that my van had been towed. I broke into tears.

*

I got a call from my daughter about eleven that night.

"I hear it has been a hard day for you," she said. Her smoky voice sounded strained and tired.

"Shaneika Mary Todd, I suppose," I replied.

"Yes." A long pause. "I've placed her on retainer. You don't have to worry about a thing."

"I am sorry about this. It hasn't been in the papers yet, but . . ."

"I know," she said, cutting me off. "Don't worry about me. I have had worse press."

"You know, Ms. Todd is too subtle for this case. I think we need to get someone more aggressive."

My daughter laughed. "She's quite the barracuda."

"Apparently, Ms. Todd thinks the interview was a disaster. She chewed me up pretty good."

"I don't think it's as bad as that. Shaneika just wanted to scare you away from cooperating with the police. I think she made it sound worse than it really is."

"I hope you are right."

"That's why she's the best in town. If we need more fire power, we will branch out nationally, but I doubt we will need it."

"What's the deal with the British accent?"

"She was raised in Bermuda but her family is from Lexington."

Before I could comment, there was a clicking on the line. I knew our time was up.

"I'll be keeping an eye on this. Don't worry," she said before hanging up the phone.

I turned over in the bed, pulling the covers around me. It was quite some time before I fell asleep.

6

I spent the next few days holed up in my home cleaning and cooking, which is what I do when feeling wounded. I washed the bulletproof windows, cleaned my comfort toilets and steamed the Italian-made tile floors. The house was designed to blend in with the elements of earth, wind, fire and water. Built in the eighties, it had been a state-of-the-art environmental house girdled by solar panels, moats, water collection and cisterns. Intended to act as a living organism within nature, it created a new style of a cradle-to-the-grave house. Even as the inconvenience of aging accumulated, one could live hassle free. Other than having a child, it was my supreme contribution to the world. One that I hoped would live long after me.

There are four iconic twentieth-century homes in the U.S. that are works of art. There's the Farnsworth House on Fox River in Illinois, Phillip Johnson's Glass House in New Canaan, Connecticut, and Frank Lloyd Wright's Fallingwater House in Bear Run Nature Preserve, Pennsylvania. The other is mine – the Butterfly.

I tenderly patted the limestone wall of my home. Its four major building components – local limestone, Kentucky walnut and oak, reinforced concrete and walls of bulletproof glass – shield me from drunken poachers shooting across the river. The house still has a futuristic look, even by today's standards.

The most distinctive feature – a second roof – consists of two distinct etched metal wings that meet at a copper gutter that cascades rainwater. As the second roof is not attached to the house-proper except by pipes, it stands on steel legs, giving it extra height. The purpose of the extra shield is two-fold: to collect rainwater and create a stunning water feature. Every minute of the day, a steady stream of water thunders twenty feet off the roof via the gutter into a rock basin surrounded by ferns. The water is gathered again and pushed upwards by an ancient corroded pump that acts as a heartbeat to the house. Budda-bump. Budda-bump. Budda-bump.

The collected water feeds not only the heated pool, but also other water features such as a fish-filled moat surrounding the house. As the pool and moat fill, rainwater spills into three cisterns that are the source of water for the house via an antique chlorine purifying system. During droughts, I simply borrow water from the pool.

Solar panels, still blanketing the side yard, provide some electricity, but they have become worn with age. As backup, a generator did supplement the house's electrical needs but only Brannon knew how to maintain it. After he left, I reluctantly connected with the city's power company.

For whimsy, I had a local artist weld two large metal antennae to the top of the roofline. From a distance, the house seems to be taking flight like a giant moth. Brannon thought it made the house look ridiculous. Looking back now, I wish I hadn't done it. It caused a breach between Brannon and me.

Unfortunately, my dwelling has begun to acquire a run-down appearance. I no longer let people see her in her present condition. Oh yes, it is a she - most definitively.

While still impressive with her roof waterfall, freestanding swivel closets, and kitchen space with dramatic clean minimal lines, the house looked shabby. I had no idea how I was going to get the lady back on her feet.

And now people were coming by uninvited. Fired up to get better security, I dipped into my meager retirement fund and installed monitors in my beeyard plus a new security system throughout the house. A new electronic gate guards my property's entrance. It was something I should have done a long time ago, but I had always felt safe as I was tucked away on the steep palisades of the Kentucky River.

As an added precaution, I secreted tasers throughout the house. I own a handgun, which my daughter purchased for me, but its cold metal frightens me. The use of a gun is so final, while the taser brings on only a very bad headache and a lawsuit. I'd rather deal with a lawsuit than a dead person, so it is my weapon of choice.

I was now forty thousand dollars poorer. That amount did not include the purchase of a fawn-colored English mastiff puppy named Baby or the cost of his future guard training . . . or the vast amounts of food he chows down . . . or my fifties era couch I would have to replace after he finished gnawing it to bits. Other than that, things were going just swell.

After pushing all the little buttons I needed to arm the security system, I took my glass filled with bourbon onto the limestone terrace shiny from wear, and fell back into an oversized chair. I sipped the golden liquid while listening to the birds. The view from this spot never failed to grab my heart. *This is my house.* My husband built it, but it was designed to my specifications and desires. Everything I knew about art, style and nature was poured into these walls. The Butterfly was his greatest triumph, but Brannon never liked it. He preferred his antebellum houses. After a while, he did not live at the Butterfly even though we were never officially separated.

I pushed that thought from my mind, as it was ancient history. I needed to concentrate on the present. The new puppy was asleep at my feet. Some puppy. He was only ten weeks old but already weighed twenty-five pounds, and his paws were the size of my hands. His breathing showed the pattern of deep, contented sleep while his potbelly went up and down like a water-pump handle. I rubbed his soft tan fur with my big toe while reaching for a legal pad and pencil.

My problem was that I agreed with the police. I didn't think Richard's death was just an accident. Why was Richard on my property? What was his mode of transportation? Someone had to have been with him to remove the vehicle. Why did the bees sting a bee-charmer? I had seen Richard work with bees. They loved him. He was never stung, even when covered with the critters. Something or someone made those bees sting him. Still – it could have been a case of Richard wanting to vandalize my hives and having a heart attack, then falling into the hive. His accomplice ran off, not wanting to be implicated. If Richard had had a heart attack, wouldn't the accomplice have helped him to the ground and tried CPR while calling 911? Or did the accomplice leave before Richard had his attack? It was the vandalism with which I had the most trouble. It just didn't seem like

Richard's style. He loved direct confrontation. Sneakiness was not his MO.

I jotted down my thoughts. I had three different theories: sex, money, and revenge. They were the cause of most murders. I needed to find out which one had led to his death.

Matt called after each workday. I think he needed to be reassured himself. Matt seemed perturbed especially after the *Herald-Leader* published the story. Luckily, it just mentioned my name in connection with the location, and said that determination of death was still to be determined. No mention of foul play.

I received several calls from my fellow beekeepers trying to worm out details, but I played dumb. I did welcome one interesting call from Irene Meckler, who sold sunflowers at the Farmers' Market. She had been a member for twenty-five years and knew where all the bodies were buried, so to speak.

"Josiah, honey, I'm sorry to bother you but I didn't know if I would be seeing you soon at the Market."

"What can I do you for?" I asked, a little guardedly.

"I don't need to know what happened at your place . . ."

"Nothing that I had a hand in, Irene, I assure you."

"Well, this has been preying on my mind. Thought you should know. About twelve years back, I found Tellie in a tearful tizzy sitting in her car at the Market. Richard had gone to wet his whistle with several other farmers and left Tellie alone to tear down the booth. Isn't that just like Richard to let Tellie, all by herself, tear down that stuff . . ."

"Why was she crying?" I interrupted.

"That's what I am trying to get at. How do I say this nicely? You know Taffy, their daughter, is not the sharpest knife in the drawer, God bless her heart."

"Yeah." I wished Irene would get to the point.

"Taffy was only seven then and was not doing well in school. Tellie had her . . . what you call it . . . evaluated that week. Honey, the test results were not good. Oh, I don't mean she has the IQ of an idiot but Tellie is so smart, she thought Taffy would be too."

I wondered where this was going.

"Tellie blamed Richard. Said he hit her when she was pregnant and she believed that incident caused some problem with Taffy."

"Goodness! So, is Taffy . . . slow? I though she just had learning disabilities."

"Naw, she gets letters backwards when she reads and has very little common sense just like most of humanity, but that's all. I think mostly Taffy just would not apply herself. I always thought Tellie expected too much of her. Not everyone can exceed like Tellie did at schoolwork. But Richard hitting a pregnant woman – that's just lowdown dirty. Yes, indeedy, I told Tellie that she should have tried to kill the old coot like his first wife did."

"Richard had a first wife?"

"Agnes Bledsoe from Pike County. Her people are hill folk and have a fierce reputation, even up in the hollers. They're known to carry pistols, even the women."

"Still?"

"You betcha."

"Tell me all the details. I am riveted."

"Agnes is a dark-headed woman with Cherokee blood. They met at Morehead College and came back to Lexington after they were hitched. He was crazy in love with Agnes. Things seemed good for them. They went to the same church as I did, which is how I first knew them. Richard had a job with IBM making good money, plus his bees, while Agnes stayed home waiting to get pregnant. The only hitch was that Agnes loved to dance. Every Saturday, she and Richard would go out. That is where the trouble started, I reckon. Agnes' good looks invited comments from other men, making Richard crazy. He would get in a fight, spoiling Agnes' fun – then they'd fight. It really put a strain on their marriage."

"Did she egg Richard's fighting on?"

"Perhaps. She was young, pretty and full of spit and vinegar. She certainly was testing the waters to see how far she could push him. Maybe by this time, she tired of him and wanted to spread her wings a little bit, started lookin' 'round. The one thing I do know for sure is that one day while reading the paper, I came across an article stating that Agnes had been arrested for the attempted murder of Richard. Said she tried to stab him."

"What happened?" I was writing furiously on my legal pad.

"Apparently charges were dropped. Richard never spoke of it. Agnes stopped coming around the Market. Never heard another thing about it except to read about the final divorce decree in the paper. Richard was always very secretive about his life. Several years later, Tellie was introduced as the new wife."

"And lots younger than Richard. Fits the male mid-life crises pattern."

"Sure do. Thought you might want to know."

"Thanks, Irene. It fills in some holes. Do you know what happened to Agnes?"

"You betcha. She owns her own company that does PR work for the horse industry and has a house in the gated area of Hartland subdivision."

"You know, I might want to talk with her. Does she go by Pidgeon?"

"Thought you might want to chew the fat with her. She took back her maiden name."

"Do you know the name of her company?"

"I think it is just listed under her name. Very dignified. Very discreet. I don't think she even hangs out a sign. Just word of mouth."

"Wow. Thanks, Irene. I'll see what I can find out." I hung up and formulated a plan. I would have a better chance of speaking with Agnes Bledsoe at work, so I called my buddies who worked in the Thoroughbred industry and asked around. It seemed that Agnes had become a high muckety-muck in the marketing world of horses. I learned that she was very good and even respected overseas. She was also very expensive and so exclusive that her phone number was not even listed. I was impressed. How many businesses go out of their way to hide themselves? Agnes had bought a historical building downtown, refurnished it and located her office there many years ago. I had always thought the building was a private residence but it was really the busy factory of Agnes Bledsoe, making her filthy rich.

I called but was told that I could not have an appointment with her. I don't know upon what basis the snotty jerk of a receptionist made that decision. Maybe she had a phone ID that gave people's bank account amount when calling. Seeing Miss Agnes was going to call for some ingenuity, so I decided to become creative. Getting transferred to Agnes's secretary, I made an appointment for the next day by telling the young woman that I was working on a story for *Southern Living*. I was surprised she believed me. I'm usually a terrible liar, but since my fanny was put in a iron skillet with the fire turned on high, I guess my skill had improved.

7

Arriving early at the immaculate grounds of Agnes Bledsoe's business address, I was made to wait just a few minutes before being shown into a dark, paneled office with a splendid view of the old Grecian-styled Carnegie library. The office reeked of cigar smoke, bourbon whiskey and Lemon Pledge – my favorite smells – so go figure. Silver trophies and plaques graced polished shelves as oil paintings of famous horse champions hung on the walnut paneled walls.

Agnes Bledsoe was everything I expected. Even in her mid-sixties, Agnes was quite a looker with her Native American heritage much in evidence – high cheekbones, ruddy skin tones and beautiful dark hair that I was sure had never seen a dye bottle. As she rose from her desk, she buttoned her Ann Taylor navy jacket that had a tease of a peach silk camisole peeking out. Her gold jewelry was modest but expensive. I noticed she still wore a wristwatch. Most people don't now because of cell phones.

I glanced haplessly at my out-of-date wool skirt sporting a healthy crop of lint balls. Mud was caked on the heels of my ankle boots. Fearing that I was going to leave dirt on her Persian carpet, I inwardly groaned.

Agnes shook my hand with a crisp grip while telling her secretary to bring us tea.

As soon the door closed, I blurted out my confession. "Ms. Bledsoe, I am so sorry, but I am here under a pretext," I babbled. "I didn't know if you would see me knowing the real reason for my visit."

"You're not one of those PETA people, are you?" asked Agnes, alarmed.

"No. I'm here about Richard Pidgeon."

Agnes took in a sharp breath. "You look familiar. I know who you are. You're Josiah Reynolds, the UK art professor. I heard one of your lectures at the Newman Center on traditional symbolism in religious paintings during the Dark Ages."

"I no longer work for UK, but thank you for remembering me."

"Nothing to thank me about. I thought you were perfectly dreadful. Didn't understand a damn thing you said."

Okay – if this is the way she wants to play. A soft knock on the door kept me from responding. Her secretary brought in an ancient tea service and set it down on the coffee table. Agnes gestured to the surrounding chairs. I plopped down immediately.

Agnes settled in a moss green camelback settee and began serving tea with perfect aplomb. I nervously rested the nineteenth century china cup on an end table, fearful that I might splatter tea on her antique furniture. As I had already lied to the woman, I certainly didn't want to leave a water spot on her Duncan Phyfe. Agnes watched me the way a cat watches a fluttering bird. "I must say you have my curiosity.

Why here about Richard? I divorced him years ago."

"If you know who I am, then you must know that Richard died on my property . . ."

Agnes gaped at me with genuine shock and her hand faltered. I quickly grabbed her tilting teacup. She sputtered something unintelligible. Seeing a bottle of water on her desk, I fetched it for her. I was about to call her secretary when she regained her composure. Mopping her forehead with a tea towel, she said, "My, my! Aren't you the jack-in-the-box of bad news. First you lie to get into my office and now you bring death to my door. How else may I be of help to you, Mrs. Reynolds?"

"Are you telling me that you didn't know that Richard had died?"

"Richard and I don't have mutual friends. I don't read the paper unless it is the racing news. No, I didn't know. How did he . . . pass away?"

I briefly told her the circumstances of his death.

"I still don't see why you are here."

"There are some questions about his death. Since he died on my property, I am seeking information that might answer them."

Agnes Bledsoe was a sharp woman. "So there are some questions about his death and now you are here trying to find something that could pin Richard's death on me. Aren't you a plum!"

My face blushed. With my flyaway red hair and freckles, I knew I must have looked most unattractive and guilty.

"I haven't been married to Richard for over two decades but I keep ..." She stopped talking to wipe her running nose "I kept tabs on him from time to time through a private detective. I couldn't risk personal contact with him, but I wanted to know how he was doing. You see, I loved Richard Pidgeon and never stopped."

Talk about being hit over the head. I was stunned. How could this beautiful, accomplished woman love a piece of manure like Richard Pidgeon?

"I can see by your face that you didn't expect this. When I met Richard in college, he was handsome, witty and lots of fun. We fell in love, got married and moved to Lexington. Everything was fine. I even overlooked his little obsessions about routine and cleanliness."

"What do you mean by 'his little obsessions'?"

"At first, I thought it was just his prissy nature. It wasn't terribly noticeable, just odd things here and there. The yard had to be just right. He wouldn't wear shirts that weren't starched . . . things like that. We had a good first five years together. Then the car accident happened. It was on a Saturday night, and we were going to the Holiday Inn to hear JD Crowe. A drunk hit us, pretty badly. Totaled the car. Richard was in severe pain for a long time."

Agnes glanced down at her perfect manicure. "It was then that his compulsiveness began to surface. He was restless, impatient with any imperfection whether it be at work or just having his handkerchiefs not being ironed to his specifications. People began to annoy him more and more.

"We both thought it was his pain medication, so we had the doctor fiddle with the dosage. That didn't work. Richard was becoming as concerned as I was, but couldn't seem to control his moods. He became more and more explosive. Finally, we resorted to seeing a therapist. Richard was diagnosed with OCD."

"Obsessive compulsive disorder," I stated.

"Yes." Agnes nodded. "At that time, there were few

medications for his problem and what was available made him sick. We tried talk therapy but it did little good. The therapist felt that Richard had a genetic predisposition to OCD and the car accident had made it worse. It could have been from either a chemical change in his brain or chronic fear the accident had instilled in him. It didn't matter. For three years we went from one treatment to the next. Nothing worked, and we were running out of options as Richard became more controlling and abusive."

"By abusive, do you mean violent?"

"He slapped me twice. On the third slap, I took a fire poker to his head."

I handed Agnes the newspaper article about her arrest from what was then the *Lexington Herald*, which I had copied at the library. She read the copy with detachment.

Agnes cleared her throat. "This is wrong. I didn't try to stab him. I hit him with a poker. The charges were dropped. Richard came to jail to collect me, but I wouldn't go with him. My mind was already made up. I told Richard I was going to divorce him. As much as I loved him, I loved myself more. I told him that we would eventually ruin each other. He would hit me again one day and, on that day, I would kill him. It was best that we part."

"How did he take it?"

"Hard, very hard." She glared at me with barely concealed contempt. "I know what Richard had become, but deep down he was a decent man, a good man. He didn't ask for what happened to him. It was something out of his control. At one time Richard was a young man full of promise. If that drunk hadn't hit us, maybe Richard would never have become an irritable, selfish man. Who are you to judge him?"

I didn't want to cause Agnes Bledsoe any more pain, so I

mumbled a thank you and left with my hat in my hand, so to speak. I sat in my van near Gratz Park scribbling notes about our conversation on my legal pad. I tried to mentally justify the fact that I had lied and caused pain to another person. It was obvious to me that Agnes Bledsoe had once deeply loved Richard and still did. Still, whether from my stubbornness or anger at her thinly veiled insults, I wrote her name down as a possible suspect. Someone drove Richard to my house. Could it have been Agnes?

*

Arriving home before dusk, I checked on my various grazing pets such as rescued racehorses that freely wandered my 139 acres. I tossed apples along the winding gravel road for the goats. Coming to my beeyard, I parked the van.

Honeybees flitted through the open windows of the van, some of them lighting on my arms so they could groom or collect pollen from their bodies. It was a shame that the furry insects would not allow themselves to be petted. People would like them better if they could stroke the bees' downy little heads. Sitting in my rusty van, I watched the bees until twilight passed – thinking, thinking, thinking.

8

The following Saturday, I went to work at the Farmers' Market, putting on a brave front. The morning went by quickly. Before I knew it, I had sold out all of my award-winning Locust Honey. It seemed that people had read the article about the incident and were interested in checking me out. That was fine with me as long as they purchased something. I was handing a customer her order of Wildflower Honey when Detective Goetz materialized at my booth. His sudden appearance startled me. He was decked out in a blue T-shirt that sported "WILDCAT COUNTRY" and a pair of out-of-season, black plaid Bermuda shorts. A small patch of a pale, hairy paunch peeped from beneath his shirt. Thank goodness he knew enough not to wear socks with his sandals.

"Detective, I'm afraid I am not allowed to talk to you without Ms. Todd," I said peevishly. I was irritated that he would bother me at work.

Responding with a sheepish grin, he said, "Thought I'd come down and see what you did." Goetz whistled appreciatively. "Look at all this honey. I love honey, you know. Big fan." He tapped his chest. "Good for your heart."

I relaxed somewhat. "I have some Wildflower Honey left or perhaps you would like a honey with lemon oil added to it. Great for putting in your tea."

Goetz laid his bag of heirloom tomatoes on my table and perused all my different honeys. "How come the honey is different colors?"

"Well, the color, texture and taste depend of the plant nectar the bee has harvested. Plant nectar can produce honey that is different in taste and color. For example, the white Dutch clover plant will produce a mild yellow honey we know as clover while the buckwheat plant will produce a honey that is almost black and tastes like molasses."

"I had no idea," he said, holding up various bottles to the sun.

"Yes, customers are always surprised to learn that the United States produces over 300 different varieties of honey while Kentucky produces over thirty."

"Which honey is the best?"

"There is no best. It's all personal preference. Some people like mild honeys while others like very strong tasting honeys."

"I'm afraid of bees," he confessed.

"Most people are," I replied. I understand since I am afraid of wasps myself."

"So . . . you actually make a living from doing this?" Goetz asked.

I acted as though I didn't hear him.

Goetz finally got the message. "Right," he said to himself. "Can I ask you something?"

"Ask away," I answered while applying labels to bottles of honey.

"You get stung much?"

I put down my bottle and gave Goetz my best look of annoyance. "Of course I do. I am a beekeeper. Mr. Goetz, why are you here?"

"Detective," he insisted as he rubbed his chin. Just as Goetz started to speak again, Matt popped up from behind my booth.

"Hello," he said, looking between Detective Goetz and me. "If it isn't the esteemed Detective Goetz."

Goetz gathered his tomatoes. "Nice to see you both again." He shambled off.

Matt watched him intently as the detective disappeared into the crowd. "What was that about?"

"I really don't know."

"Ooooh, Josiah, maybe he thinks he can win your trust and make you confess over some rum cocktails," Matt teased.

"Confess what?" I replied in a voice that was a little too loud.

Matt laughed heartily as he leaned over and pinched my arm. His black hair shimmered in the sunlight. "The murder, old girl, the murder. I put my money on you knocking off the old buzzard out of pure spite."

"Well, aren't you very cheeky today." I lowered my voice as I leaned closer to Matt. "I know that I am supposed to be sad, but the truth is I am glad Pidgeon is dead."

Matt's handsome face suddenly crumbled as though he remembered that he had forgotten to turn off the stove. Motioning me to be quiet, he went around the front of the table and felt under the yellow plastic tablecloth. He yanked a small black plastic microphone from the bottom of the table and held it up. We both looked at each other in astonishment.

I had just damned myself. Snatching the device from Matt's hand, I rushed into the crowd. Frantically scanning for Goetz, I spotted him a block down tasting goat's cheese samples. I caught up with him, grabbed his massive arm and swung him around. His craggy face registered surprise, then embarrassment as I brandished the microphone. He pulled an earphone out of his ear.

I waved the device in his face. "This is over the top and you know it. You better have a warrant for this."

He reached out for the microphone, but I quickly thrust it between my ample bosoms. "Oh no. My lawyer gets this first. So you want to know why I hated Pidgeon?"

Detective Goetz was quick to recover. "Yeah, I would like to know why a respectable, hardworking woman would show so much emotion about a man she supposedly wasn't involved with."

"Involved with?" I laughed bitterly. "You guys are barking up the wrong tree. Besides being a liar and a cheat, Pidgeon was a woman beater. Check the local hospitals' ER records and then talk to his wife. If anyone had a motive to kill Pidgeon, it was Tellie, his wife."

"You know this first hand? You've seen Mrs. Pidgeon being hit or she told you about it?"

"I know this from my own observation. Something you and your partner should try a little more of. She often showed up at the Market with bruises."

"Miss Josiah," he said, "it has been my life experience that observation often means little or nothing without corroboration. Things are never quite what they seem from the outside looking in. As far as you know, she could be just clumsy or be in the first stages of MS or have inner ear problems. You just have a theory without proof." He looked away. "Are you done?" Goetz seemed offended and wanted to be shed of me.

"What do you think you have on me? You have no physical evidence to tie me with Pidgeon's death, yet you keep hounding me. I had nothing to do with that man's demise." We stood facing each other like wary catamounts. Finally, fearing that I would be blamed for tampering with police equipment, I handed Goetz his listening device. He at least had the good manners to blush. The bug was really over the top and he knew it. This wasn't the crime of the century.

I shifted my weight. The arthritis was starting to burn in my legs. "Yes we are done, I hope for good."

"Okay."

"Okay, you believe me and will leave me alone?"

"Okay in meaning that I got your message." His features slackened. "I'm not the enemy."

I took a deep breath. "Yes, you are," I replied before I turned and melted into the street crowd. I had to walk seven blocks before I found a pay phone. My legs were on fire from all the walking. I dialed a number that my daughter had had me memorize. I reached an old-fashioned, answering service. I said only one word before I hung up – "Rosebud."

9

I needed to push this investigation away from me. Though I was sure I would never be convicted, a murder trial would ruin me financially, costing me everything I had managed to squirrel away. I needed to determine who wanted Pidgeon dead. Still fuming over Goetz's little trick that morning, I decided to visit Otto Brown. He was Pidgeon's booth neighbor at the Farmers' Market. Maybe he would know something.

The foot traffic at the Market was slowing, so I decided to take a break as it was getting close to the end of the selling day. Some farmers were currently packing up and dismantling their tents. Hiding my cash box in the van, I put a fifty in my pocket and strolled down the median to Otto Brown's booth. While waiting for his customers to finish their transactions, I picked out some Cherokee Purple tomatoes. After patiently waiting my turn, I offered my selections to Otto to weigh.

"How's the day been?"

"Fair to middlin'," Otto said, putting the tomatoes

carefully in a bag. He scratched his unshaven cheek as he eyed the scale. I didn't know how he could see the scales from the large eyebrows fingering across his forehead and others caught in his long eyelashes. He would have had pretty eyes except for the hair jungle above his eyeballs.

"It's been slow my way too," I replied trying to establish eye contact with him.

He didn't look up from his tasks.

"I suppose you know that your next door buddy was found dead on my property."

"Talk is he died from heart failure."

"That's right." I could tell Otto wanted me to leave. He kept turning his back to me. I leaned forward. "Otto, did Richard ever tell you that he was gonna mess with my hives? Anything like that?"

"Can't rightly say."

Losing my patience, I blurted out, "Oh, for gaawwd sakes, Otto, he trashed your tomatoes every chance he got. Said you bought them from a terminal in Lincoln County. You are not going to lose any brownie points by telling me the truth. Now – did he ever say anything about me?" I slid the fifty towards him.

Otto bristled at the accusation that his tomatoes were not grown by him and stopped arranging them on the table. "Well, now, he didn't like you, Josiah. Nope, not a'tall. Said you had no business bein' here as you was rich. That you was takin' business from real beekeepers."

I laughed bitterly. "Go on."

"Never said nuthin' exactly 'bout what he might do but that you best be aware."

"Be aware of what?"

"Well, of him, I 'spect." Otto pulled a tobacco pouch from his pocket and shoved a big wad in his mouth. He had a paper cup that he used as a spittoon. *Yuck.*

"When did he say that?"

"Couple weeks ago."

"Why didn't you tell me he was gunning for me?"

"'Tis none of my business. Besides I'd be tellin' ya somethin' you probably knew," said Otto.

"Geez, Otto, you good old boys sure stick together," I said.

Otto pursed his lips and spat in his cup. "Richard was no good ol' boy. He was city. Lived in town. Used other folks' land to farm his bees. No, Richard was a townie. Not one of us."

When I decided I wasn't going to get any more out of Otto, I left him my fifty and carried a large box of beautiful Cherokee Purple tomatoes to my booth. Otto may be a throwback to the nineteenth century, but he sure knew how to grow heirloom tomatoes. I had no idea what I was going to do with all those tomatoes. Guess I could make a huge batch of salsa. Matt loved salsa. But at least I had discovered that there was smoldering resentment from one older farmer against landless members in the Market. Interesting.

As I walked back to my booth, I spied Pidgeon's daughter, Taffy, going from booth to booth, apparently wringing out the last bit of sympathy she could. I wondered if she was talking about me. Or was I just being paranoid? By the aversion of vendors' eyes as I passed by, I guess being paranoid was correct in this instance.

I had gotten used to being the center of people's attention for a long time, ever since my husband became a nationally known architect. I had learned to deal with the curious, the well-intended and the envious who were determined to be hurtful. I stiffened when Taffy approached my booth. Which would she be?

"Mornin', Miss Josiah," she said.

"Hello Taffy," I replied, aware that the other farmers were watching from the corners of their eyes. "My condolences for the loss of your father."

"Miss Josiah, I won't play the grieving daughter if you won't play the concerned friend."

"Okay."

"We both know Daddy was a big turd," she continued, inhaling deeply. "I feel like I can breathe for the first time. You did us a favor."

"I didn't do anything, either for you or to your father."

Taffy pouted. Like Detective O'nan, she didn't like being corrected. But then – who did? "Whatever. I just came by to say no hard feelings."

I decided to change the subject. "What are you and your mother going to do now?"

"Well, Mommy is still stunned. She doesn't know what to do without Daddy barking orders at her at all hours. She'll snap out of it as soon as she gets the insurance check."

"It is lucky that your father had such a large policy," I said trying to find out how much.

"How do you know how much it's for?" Taffy quizzed while readjusting her purse strap on her shoulder. Her heavily made-up brown eyes narrowed.

I shrugged. "People talk. Say it's for a million."

Taffy guffawed. "I wish." She pulled her badly dyed blond hair into a scrunchy.

"I know money can never replace a loved one, but it can soften the blows that come after."

Taffy smiled. I hoped that she would spend some of that money on dental repair. "I'll tell Mommy about your concerns." She checked the time on her cell phone. "Gotta go. You take care now, Miss Josiah."

"Will do," I said. I watched her leave in a new Prius. So Taffy was already spending the money before her mother got the check. I would have to find out more about Richard Pidgeon's life insurance policy.

10

It was a day for relentless surprises. Arriving home from the Market, I came upon three cop cars waiting at my newly installed gate. I called Shaneika immediately on my cell phone. She was incommunicado so I left a message. Ignoring O'nan as he tapped on my van window, I called Matt as well. O'nan, red-faced, was yelling at me to lower my window and waving a piece of paper in his hand.

I cranked the van window open. "What's this all about?" I asked.

Detective O'nan shoved the paper into my lap. "Warrant to search your house and property."

"The bug didn't work, so you are on another fishing trip, Detective? Don't you guys ever take a break from harassing people? We are going to sit right here until I hear from my lawyer."

O'nan sneered, showing very uniform teeth, the kind that only result from braces. "In that case, I am placing you under arrest for resisting an officer."

I was seething now. "You wouldn't dare!" I glared at O'nan. His blue eyes were lit up kind of crazy. It was my first inkling that his behavior was more than a good cop/bad cop game with Goetz. Maybe he personally disliked me, and would try to take it to the next level to see me take a hit.

Goetz was leaning against a police cruiser looking uncomfortable. From his body language, I assumed the warrant was O'nan's idea all the way down the line. But I knew he would not interfere with whatever O'nan did.

It is not unheard of around here for a suspect's head to get busted open for "resisting." For some reason, I didn't think O'nan would have any qualms arresting . . . or even tasing me. I realized I hated him . . . because I feared him.

"Okay," I said. "I always want to cooperate with the law, but I will be present and taping the entire search."

O'nan started to object, but closed his mouth. There was really nothing he could fuss about. I was within my legal rights to tape them searching my house. Climbing into the back of my rusty van, I retrieved a video camera I kept in the case of a car accident. I began by giving the date and time plus all the officers' names. Turning off my camera, I punched in the code for the gate. I went in first and drove slowly, not wanting the police to accidentally hit any of my animals, which for the most part ran free on the property. I was also stalling for time. A cruiser behind me blew its siren to move some peacocks out of its way. There were deer munching on fruit from a plum tree. They gave a disdainful look at the intruders before jumping over the pasture fence and escaping into the woods.

The warrant gave O'nan the right to search my house and property for Pidgeon's missing vehicle and epinephrine pens. The pens gave me a clue. Every beekeeper keeps one handy in case he gets one bee sting too many and goes into anaphylactic shock. Epinephrine, which is nothing more than adrenaline, will save a life. It usually comes in a tube with a springboard needle that thrusts through clothes into the thigh. They are called adrenaline or adi pens for short. Yet, a dose of epinephrine can cause a heart attack if the heart is weak. A glimmer of an idea took root in my mind.

Once we got to the house, the entourage of cops waited for me to punch in the code for the home security system. I took this opportunity to warn them. "Guys, you break it, you pay for it. Understand."

O'nan just grimaced. I looked about for Goetz but didn't see him. I watched a cadre of young policemen with military haircuts spread out through my property. Their faces revealed a childlike excitement as though they were about to hunt for Easter eggs. Deep in my heart, I worried they would plant evidence.

I keyed in the code to the house, and opened the steel front door letting the police pass into the main hallway. Almost every one had the same expression – one of awe. The waterfall cascading off the roof into a rock-hewn basin, the moats filled with water plants, the exposed steel frames, the wooden beams, the large expanse of glass overlooking the river and the artwork, which had taken me a lifetime to collect, hanging on the concrete walls. One cop popped his gum and whistled in admiration.

O'nan waved his hand getting their attention. He separated them into groups of two. It would be hard for me to keep up with them as they were going through my things. I resumed my recording.

O'nan sidled up to me. "Mrs. Reynolds, do you have any adrenaline injections?"

"Yes, I do. I also have the prescription for them. I can account for each and every one of my injections."

"I will need a copy of your prescription."

"I can get that and more." I went to a writing pad and wrote my doctor's number on it while hearing closet doors opening and furniture being pulled out. I handed the paper to O'nan and then resumed recording. The ransacking of my house went on for twenty minutes. My paintings were torn from the walls and sculptures turned upside down. Suddenly, I heard a crash in the other room. Running into the library, I found a horrified cop clutching an early Stephen Powell glass piece.

"I am sorry. It slipped. I think the neck is cracked," said the officer, his face clouded with dismay. He was truly mortified. Even so he had just damaged an important piece of art.

Turning towards O'nan, I could barely control the anger in my voice. "That is a $30,000 Stephen Powell work. It is a one-of-a-kind piece of hand-blown art glass. Now it's ruined," I protested.

O'nan glanced at it. "Put some glue on it. No one will notice."

"You crazy fu . . . " I said when my cell phone interrupted me. It was Shaneika. I hurriedly told her what was going on. She told me to put O'nan on the phone.

"Unhuh," he said, picking lint off his pants. "Unhuh. Nope. Okay." O'nan handed the phone back to me. "Let's wind this up," he called out to his minions, waving a finger in the air. He then turned towards me, "You can file a report about that glass and see if the city will pay for it. Just call the Department."

The commotion had awakened Baby, who was now

whimpering in his crate. I let him out, but before I could grab him, he rushed over to O'nan. Growling, he tried to protect me by placing himself between O'nan and me. Unfortunately, in his excitement he piddled right in front of O'nan. "Great watchdog you got there," said O'nan, stepping back from the puddle. I picked Baby up and cradled his squirming body. He smothered my face with puppy kisses while still dripping droplets of urine.

"Yeah, well, he knows who's responsible for this mess. Can't you go now and leave us in peace?"

O'nan rounded up his men and was gone. It had taken less than thirty minutes to destroy a $30,000 art piece and ransack my home. It had made O'nan's day, but I was sorely pissed.

*

Several hours later Shaneika arrived and found Matt and me in my office going through boxes of records from my years of teaching at UK. Baby was happily chewing on a toy in Matt's lap. "You sure got some crazy-ass art in this weird house of yours," remarked Shaneika. "Is that a George Nakashima that you are using for a dining room table?"

"I am surprised that a homegirl would recognize a George Nakashima," murmured Matt, thumbing through some old correspondence.

Shaneika grimaced. "Well, I'm sure you would know – a stylista like yourself," she responded with a lisp and a limp wrist.

"Speaking of being a stylista, how's that Billy Idol haircut working out for you?" asked Matt.

"Bite me," retorted Shaneika.

66

"I found it!" I cried. "I knew I had seen our buddy O'nan somewhere before." Matt scooted closer so he could read off my lap as Shaneika grabbed a chair.

"In 1989, O'nan took one of my classes with several of his jock buddies. An easy A or so he thought. He was on a baseball scholarship. Well, the class was harder than he had anticipated. I caught O'nan and his baseball pals cheating on a test. Here is the letter about it to the dean, his coach and his scholarship sponsor."

Shaneika's eyes brightened. "I can do a lot with this," she said, perusing the letters. "Especially with what I found out today." She beamed triumphantly. "It seems that Pidgeon's heart attack was possibly caused by too much adrenaline pumped into his system. They found two weird looking puncture points on his neck but can't positively say they weren't bee stings. The working theory is that someone injected the adrenaline rush and then used the bee stings to cover up the wounds."

"Adrenaline like from an epinephrine injector or pen," nodded Matt.

"But because of all the bee stings they really can't identify a point of entry, not so that it will legally stand up in a court of law."

"So they have no weapon, no vehicle, no point of entry of the adrenaline into the body," I said.

"In other words, they have a theory, but no case. No real evidence. They can't legally say it was murder. They can't find any weapon with your fingerprints on it. They don't even know how he got there," said Matt.

I thought for a moment. "Let's say they did find an adi pen with both Richard's and my fingerprints on it. Could they prove it was murder? Maybe he and I were there, and he was getting stung and having a reaction. How can they prove that I didn't give him the injection in order to save him?" I thought some more. "If he were subject to multiple bee stings, wouldn't his body produce more adrenaline anyway? How can they prove the adrenaline was from an injection and not produced by his own body?"

Shaneika looked baffled. "That better not be what happened, Miss Josiah, because that means you lied to me. If for some reason, the DA wanted to push this case that would be our defense if they could ever tie one of your pens to Pidgeon. We would probably plead it down to manslaughter."

"I didn't lie," I assured Shaneika. "I'm just thinking out loud. Looking at all the possibilities. I am fearful of what O'nan might try in order to convince the DA. At this point, he could twist the facts into anything he liked. Besides, it seems that the point of Pidgeon showing up in my yard was to place blame on me specifically. Or else why wouldn't the killer do it in Pidgeon's own beeyard where it would look like a simple accident."

"Perhaps the murderer, and I say this with reservation as I don't really believe a murder took place, wasn't sure that the bees would sting Richard enough to cover point of adrenaline entry. Having his death in your beeyard gave the police someone specific to look at in case the medical examiner could pinpoint cause of death," countered Shaneika, reaching over to pet my mastiff. She casually wiped Baby's slobber on Matt's pants leg.

"Can you get O'nan thrown off the case?" asked Matt, smearing the slobber from his pants onto Baby's fur. "It is clear that the police have nothing concrete, but O'nan is using this incident to get back at Josiah."

"It looks pretty obvious that O'nan is using Pidgeon's death to make your life a living hell. Yeah, I can get him thrown off, and also request a review of how the case was handled," mused Shaneika. "But it will only antagonize him more."

"My experience has been that backing down from bullies only compounds the problem. No, let's hit back. I don't like him thinking I am defenseless," I said.

"Did O'nan end up losing his scholarship?" asked Matt.

"I don't know. After I kicked him out of my class, I didn't keep up with him," I said. "It didn't concern me anymore."

"Until now," said Matt.

"Until now," I concurred.

"I think we should have a victory dinner," stated Shaneika. "Just a few more nips and tucks, but basically, this nasty business is over. Miss Josiah, you are elected to cook, and then after dinner, show me around this *crazzzy* house of yours."

"I will do the cooking, if you please," corrected Matt. "Trust me, you don't want to eat hers."

I frowned. Matt seemed to be showing off for Shaneika. "You sure seem to eat a lot of my *bad* cooking."

"Feel sorry for you, that's all." He started towards the kitchen. Baby loped after him. "Also, will be staying here . . . until this is officially over. I'll be bedding down in the old caretaker's cabana."

I started to protest but Shaneika cut me off. "I think this is for the best. O'nan apparently has a vendetta against you. Anytime someone believes you ruined his life and carries a gun, you should take every precaution. O'nan is a very real danger until this mess is sorted out."

I nodded in agreement. She was right. It just unnerved me that two younger people were making better decisions than I. It made me feel old.

"I want some wine with dinner, honey child," she called after Matt. "And you, Josiah, are going to tell me how you lost all your money, but manage to still live like a rich woman," she said, training her eyes on me.

"What makes you think that I have lost my money?"

"You don't get your hair professionally done."

"Maybe I'm eccentric."

"Not it. Women your age always get their hair done. And this house needs a lot of work," Shaneika said, looking around. "You drive a thirty-plus-year-old beater and you are really worried about my fees – not that I cost you anything. Like I said, I owe your daughter a favor."

"Want to tell me about that favor?"

"Quit changing the subject. What happened to your money?"

"It's a long story," I replied.

"I've got all night. No court tomorrow. Since I saw that heated pool out back, I will be spending lots of time out here. I love to swim. You got any problems with that?"

Laughing, I held up my hands in surrender. "No, it will be fun having the house filled with young people again."

"I saw some horses when I came in."

"I rescued a couple that were starving. Sometimes when friends go out of town, I'll watch their horses for them. I don't board them as a rule."

"I like horses."

"Doesn't everyone?" I opened a carved limestone box and held it out to my lawyer. Shaneika carefully selected a cigar. We settled into our chairs to watch the sun settle over the infinity pool that blended into the Kentucky River while Matt fussed in the kitchen. Baby followed his every move, padding after him on his oversize paws, hoping that Matt would drop a morsel or two. The world was settling into night. I could hear a hoot owl combine calls with a screech owl's high-pitched ones across the river. It was peaceful, but my mind whirled up possible scenarios waiting for me. As well intended as Matt and Shaneika were, I knew this was something I had to fix . . . and fast.

After Shaneika left, Matt ensconced himself in the cabana. Knowing that Matt would be preoccupied with exploring his digs, I dressed in black, pulled my hair up into a dark hat and left the house quietly. I didn't want Matt to know where I was going. After forty minutes of driving to the north side of town, I found myself in front of Richard Pidgeon's house. There was only one light on inside. I drove past a second time to see if anyone was walking a dog or jogging at this late hour. Driving past a third time, I stopped the car. I quietly transferred all the Pidgeons' garbage from the garbage can to the back of my vehicle. I looked around again and then sped away.

When I got home, I hid the garbage bags in the tool shed. I would go through them after Matt went to work. I knew if I got caught going through the Pidgeons' garbage, it would look bad. I could only hope the garbage man came early each collection day, and Tellie and Taffy would never know that someone was stealing their garbage . . . and hopefully their secrets. Most people are too lazy to burn documents that could implicate them. They simply throw them away, thinking that the local dump will hide their sins. I knew better.

I showered and went gratefully to bed, sleeping soundly.

Awaking before noon, I found Baby in his crate where Matt had placed him. He had turned his water bowl over, and what appeared to be remnants of his breakfast stained his blanket. I let him outside, keeping a watchful eye until he tinkled. With water features surrounding the house including a deep pool, I needed to make sure that the clumsy puppy didn't fall into one of them. Baby was still learning how to walk on his oversized paws and could easily stumble on his long ears. Since he didn't want to come back inside the house, I decided that now was as good as time as any to go through the Pidgeons' garbage. Dressed in ratty cotton pj's and shoes with holes in them, I padded to the shed with Baby following. I hadn't even combed my hair yet. But it didn't matter, going through garbage. I sat in the grass with piles of rotting food and limp paper about me as Baby tried to roll in it. Finally, I had to put Baby in the tool shed so I could have some peace. I was irritated that I had forgotten gloves. After twenty-five minutes of going through nasty, stinking trash, I found nothing. Not wanting to be discovered in my theft, I burned all the paper and put the organic stuff in the compost pile, hiding it deep within.

I finally released Baby from the shed. Angered by his confinement, he would not look at me when I commanded him to follow, but sat in a stubborn hunch. "Baby, we both stink. Let's go for a swim!" Betting on his fear of abandonment, I kept walking up the gravel road. When I looked back, Baby was reluctantly following me, sniffing the ground.

Once back at the house, I pulled off my pj's and jumped in the pool. Baby excitedly barked and growled at the edge, but wouldn't come in. Finally, he lay down, resting his dark muzzle on his paws, expressive brown eyes following me. I floated on my back staring at the trees and cloudy sky. But even someone as self-centered as I am eventually gets tired of dwelling on one's problems. I climbed out of the pool, washed in the outdoor shower, ate breakfast, and cleaned the kitchen and great room. I finally got around to putting on some clothes, combed my hair and brushed my teeth.

I can't deny that I loved the freedom of my life, but I didn't feel safe anymore. I was constantly checking the security monitors. I worried about O'nan. I worried about his unchecked anger. And I worried about being the target of that anger.

The next few days went by quickly. Still, I went to collect the Pidgeons' garbage, switching it with some non-descript garbage of mine in the same type of garbage bag. It seemed like Tellie was cleaning house too, ridding herself of computer magazines, yellowing newspapers carefully folded in half, old recipes and receipts going back to 1999. I learned that Tellie liked Lean Cuisine and Cadbury bars. Her electric bill for the past two years was always thirty-two dollars and twenty-four cents. Talk about obsessive. Didn't she and Richard ever turn the lights on? I also found Tellie's pay stubs from one of the LETC Clinics in town that stayed open twenty-four/seven. Tellie had once told me that she wanted to be a pediatrician. I wondered what caused Tellie to abandon her dream of becoming a doctor and settle for being a part-time nurse at an emergency treatment center. I knew she had the brains to become a doctor. Did Richard make her quit? Maybe he wouldn't pony up the money for school. Or just maybe after she had Taffy, she wanted to stay home.

Money. That was a big issue with Richard. He was always complaining about money. It appeared that he really was having financial trouble. I found several crumpled notices from collection agencies. I also recovered a letter from the bank about the mortgage. Seems as though they had missed a few payments. A fat life insurance policy loomed larger and larger. I circled money as a motive on my legal pad.

On the eleventh day after I had started my garbage diving, I looked up from my Market booth to find Detective Goetz gazing intently at me.

"Sorry, didn't mean to startle you," he said. He was wearing what appeared to be a new sports jacket and was freshly shaved. His craggy face almost looked handsome. There was a hint of cologne drifting from him.

I was not happy to see him. I must have made a face as he tugged at his clothes saying, "Nothing up my sleeves this time."

"No invoking of the Patriot Act?" I asked.

He grinned. He had nice teeth. "I felt like a fool putting that bug on you but I was ordered to. I am only two years away from my pension, you see."

I nodded. "To what do I owe this pleasure?"

"Thought you might like to know that the medical examiner has finally ruled Pidgeon's death as accidental."

I was cautious. "And that means?"

"You are off the hook."

"Did you really think Pidgeon was murdered?"

"I thought it looked damned odd, to tell you the truth. We were given time to check out all possibilities, but none panned out. I've seen more suspicious cases turn out to be a big fat nothing. Just the wrong place at the right time."

"You didn't answer the question."

"I think what really happened is that he had his wife drive him out there to create some mischief with your hives. He had a heart attack and tumbled into the hive. Tellie lied because she didn't want to implicate herself in any trouble. Try as I could, I wasn't able to break her alibi."

"You tried to break her alibi? I bet that caused problems with O'nan."

"I never considered you seriously as a suspect. I didn't ever think you lured Pidgeon to your hives with the intention of harming him."

"But O'nan pushed it."

Goetz pursed his lips. "Detective O'nan has been placed on leave with pay for awhile. His performance on this case is being reviewed."

I pulled off my straw hat. "Detective Goetz, that is the best news I have had for weeks. Can I buy you a drink?"

"Like right now?"

"Yes, I feel like celebrating. I feel like my life has been given back to me."

"Like to, but I'm on duty. How about a rain check?"

"Okay," I said, giving him my best smile.

Goetz started to walk away but then turned. "By the way, why did you call him?"

"Who?"

"Your cell phone. Pidgeon's number really was on your cell phone log."

"I thought you and O'nan made that up. I never called him."

"Check your bill. You will find his number on it." He waved goodbye.

I now knew why Goetz came. He was making a last ditch effort to pin something on me before his buddy got the boot. That son of a bitch!

I closed up my booth early. On the way home, I called Shaneika on my cell, leaving a message. When I got home, I heard the phone ringing. I hurriedly unlocked the door and reached for the phone, "Hello?" It is a ridiculous fact of my life that my cell phone stops working in the house, causing the expense of a traditional phone.

"You sound out of breath."

"Just a minute. I gotta turn off the security system." Finishing the sequence of numbers, I plopped down. "Goetz paid me a call today. He said the case was closed."

"That's why I am calling. It was officially ruled as a heart attack, but they can still open the case again with cause," said Shaneika.

"So this is a temporary reprieve."

"Unless something pops up that makes the police want to look at the case again, I would say it is over."

"You don't sound certain."

"Nothing is certain in this world."

I frowned. "And O'nan?"

"I filed a formal complaint. I couldn't find a college picture to ID him but the socials were the same. He has been pulled off the case and is now up for a review."

"Did he lose his baseball scholarship?"

"Yes, he did. If I were you, I would cross the street if you two are ever on the same sidewalk."

"Hates me that much, huh?"

"Like a firebrand." Shaneika muffled the phone to talk with her secretary. "Back. Look, it is over. You don't owe me a thing. Like I said, I owed your daughter a favor, so you don't have to worry about that. Get on with your life. I really do think it is over for good."

"Thanks for all you did. I appreciate it," I said.

"Just make sure your daughter knows what I did for you," Shaneika replied coldly before hanging up.

Abigail Keam

11

It was one of those crisp mornings when fall was broadcasting its arrival. As usual on a Saturday, I was at the Farmers' Market peddling my honey. Every weekend the vendors supplied local meat, homegrown produce, eggs, fruit, baked goods, fish and cheese to over five thousand customers who enjoyed purchasing their food outdoors to the sounds of live music and yarns of their favorite farmer. The atmosphere was always festive.

I was placing glass honey jars in a basket when Officer Kelly rolled up on his Segway. I never failed to think of Kelly as a cliché that walked and talked. His wicked grin, his thick red hair falling over his freckled forehead causing his green eyes to peek out, and then a cop on top of that. And, of course, Irish, a descendant of immigrants who built the nineteenth-century stone fences that the tourists refer to as "slave walls."

I tried to be angry but couldn't. Officer Kelly was one of my dearest friends. He was a man who had never said an unkind word to me, who was always gallant, and who brought me food on every occasion that we saw each other. We had many things in common such as the belief that the Templar Knights still existed and the grassy knoll was overlooked in the Warren Report. Kelly introduced me to absinthe and some other bad habits about which I will never utter a word. He was a good cop, but a decadent man.

He was really my daughter's friend whom I had adopted when she moved away. Kelly was so affable, I couldn't stand to lose him so I collected him, I guess, as I did my paintings. I was there for his wedding and his children's christenings. His family and I usually had dinner once a month, but since the "incident," things had been put on hold. I hadn't seen him since this mess started with Pidgeon's death, although his wife had called several times to offer her support.

Kelly stretched out a gloved hand, which held hot chocolate and a bagel. "There is no use being mad at me, Josiah. I had to stay away, but I want you to know that I was working behind the scenes on your behalf."

"You are a liar and a coward," I replied, jerking the food out of his hands. "You cops always stick together. I'll not listen to any of your Irish glib defending your bad conduct."

"O'nan is a mean piece of work. He was watching everyone who had contact with you, especially me. But I did talk to Goetz on the sly," said Kelly.

"What did you say?"

"I said you were not the murdering type. It didn't even look like a murder case to me."

Mollified somewhat, I asked, "What did Goetz say?"

"He thought the investigation was headed in the wrong direction, but couldn't speak up because O'nan was the primary. It wasn't until your lawyer filed that petition that Goetz was able to pull free of O'nan." Kelly laughed. "Oh, man, does O'nan look like a horse's ass – getting back at his high school art teacher. He's a big joke around the station for pulling that one."

"College professor," I corrected.

"Whatever. Hey, don't be mad at me. I stood up for you."

"Who is the primary now?" I asked.

"No one. Pidgeon's death is listed as a heart attack. The medical examiner let it go."

"But it could come up again if someone pushed it?"

"Whoa, don't you know good news when you hear it?"

"Just thinking out loud. I want to know more. I know you have read the file."

"Man, don't make me," whined Kelly.

"I need help."

"But it's over."

"No, it's not. Someone is trying to put the whammy on me. Please. For old times' sake? Come on, didn't I introduce you to your wife?"

"No, you didn't, but you'll bitch to her until she makes me help you. Okay, meet me at Al's in a couple of hours. I get off my shift then," replied Kelly before speeding away on his Segway.

Al's Bar was a gritty little saloon on the corner of Sixth and Limestone where trendy urban dwellers and earnest poets hobnobbed with permanently down-and-out alcoholics. It looked like a place Hemingway would come to sip his whiskey and write a masterpiece novel. Like me, it was a little rusty around the edges, but solid at the core. At least, I liked to think so.

I got there first. Sitting in a duct-taped vinyl booth, I

asked for a Long Island iced tea. After a cheery waitress brought my drink, I ordered two cheeseburger platters with all the trimmings, knowing that Kelly would be hungry. Just as the food arrived, Kelly plopped wearily into the booth. Happily, he poured ketchup on his plate while asking the waitress for a Corona and extra napkins.

"What's it going to take for you not to be mad at me?" he asked, licking ketchup from his fingers.

"Why did the police think Pidgeon's death wasn't an accident?"

"Because it looked funny. The missing car is the main reason. If Pidgeon's car had been at your place, then we would have assumed he died while vandalizing your hives."

"But why look at me? Why not Tellie?"

Kelly took a hearty bite out of his cheeseburger and answered with his mouth full. "She was the first person they looked at, but she had an airtight alibi. Her co-worker swore that Tellie left work at her usual time at 7 a.m. Richard died around seven. Not enough time for her to drive him to your place. Tellie claims that you called Richard and that you must have picked him up. She said she drove straight home after work and went to bed. Didn't know anything until we knocked on the door."

"She's a nurse at the LETC on Tates Creek. That's only twenty minutes from me. She could have easily slipped out early," I said, grabbing some of his fries after eating all of mine.

"Couldn't shake her alibi. Like I said, with her co-worker vouching for her, and the time card punched out at the correct time, Tellie's untouchable."

"Nurses don't use time cards."

"They do at this place. New policy."

"Damn." I thought for a moment. "Who is this co-worker?"

"Name is Joyce Kramer."

"Where does she live?"

"In Meadowthorpe."

"This phone call that I supposedly made – did Tellie know for a fact that I had made it? Did she hear it?"

"She said Richard told her about it."

"So she could be telling the truth. Maybe Richard lied to her about a phone call?"

"Plausible."

"You do know that Richard might be a wife-beater."

"Of course, we heard rumors. We asked Tellie but she denied it."

"Did you check the ER records?"

"There was nothing in the file about that. O'nan was not going down that path."

"What about Taffy?"

"Never laid a hand on her that we know of."

"She could have been trying to protect her mother like Cheryl Crane killing Johnny Stompanato."

"Who?"

"You know, she killed her mother's boyfriend – her mother was the actress Lana Turner."

"Oh, movie stuff," dismissed Kelly, who thought I was too fascinated with old movies. "Taffy had an alibi with six witnesses. She had gone to a wild party the night before and passed out on her hostess' couch. Apparently, others had slept over too. She's clean."

"Any gambling debts, women?" I asked hopefully.

"Richard was a hardworking schlep with a bad temper. As far as we can tell, he was faithful to his wife, purchased everything with a debit card so he would have a written record and was obsessed with the appearance of his house and yard."

"So he wouldn't gamble because he couldn't have a written transaction of the bet."

"Exactly. You are now starting to know the man."

"I went to see Agnes, his first wife," I confessed.

Kelly seemed interested. "Agnes did not have an alibi for that morning."

"I guess it doesn't matter. She told me that she hadn't seen him since they were divorced."

"Really? According to Richard's desk calendar, they had lunch together several days before his death."

I was flummoxed. "That lying twit. And here I was feeling sorry I had bothered her. Do you know what the meeting was about?"

"She said it had to do with the divorce, a detail they had missed but she discovered while making out her will."

"What was the problem? Who is the beneficiary of the will?"

"Richard was."

"Richard?" I thought for a moment. "Did Agnes ever remarry or have kids?"

"Nope."

"Then that doesn't seem so far-fetched. She loved Richard. I don't think she really wanted to divorce him. It would make sense that she would make him her beneficiary if she has no other kin."

"But that doesn't explain why she needed to see him. She wouldn't tell O'nan. According to the case file notes, she told O'nan to go to the devil and that he was to speak to her lawyer."

I chuckled. "She is a spitfire. And she didn't tell O'nan that I had been to see her?"

"Apparently not."

"Hmmm. Maybe I should pay Agnes another call."

"Please don't, Josiah. It will come out that I talked to you. I don't want my butt on the line."

"Quit whining. I still don't think you are telling me everything."

Kelly paused for a moment. I could tell he was thinking. "Somebody keeps sending letters to the station claiming that you killed Pidgeon."

I slapped the table. Customers looked up from their booths and peered at me. "I knew someone was trying to put the whammy on me. What do the letters look like?"

"Typed."

"As in a typewriter?"

Kelly talked around his food. "Very old school." He swallowed and took a sip of his drink. "Nobody but O'nan took them seriously."

"How many are there?"

"Just two. You have picked my brain entirely. I don't know anything else. Honest. Does this even the score now?"

"You could have me over to dinner."

"That I can do."

"By the way, what happened to Goetz?"

"He has a new partner. Seems happier now." Kelly winked at me. "I think he's sweet on you."

"Really?"

"Ask him to go out with you. He'll jump at it."

I laughed. If I were going to be dating anyone, it certainly wouldn't be Goetz. I threw a twenty on the table and left Kelly with a reminder not to talk with his mouth full. He just grunted and kept chewing.

That night, I felt out of sorts. I restlessly paced the house. Matt was staying in town with his new boyfriend. Baby was in a spiteful mood, chewing on my glasses, which I had to pry from his slobbery mouth. He fought as I tried to clean his face with a washcloth. To wash the dog gunk off my hands and arms, I took a dip in the pool, noticing that the water was cool. I guess the heater was going out and I lacked the money to replace it. Was this going to be my life now? More and more things would fall into complete disrepair until I would become one of the shabby, faded gentry. The house would become a mockery of what it once was.

I had $7000 in my checking account and a $16,000 CD emergency fund. The rest of my money, which was not much, was tied up in retirement funds that would not be available for another twelve years when I turned 62.

When Brannon died, I collected his life insurance policy, which paid off the farm. I earn just enough money with the bees to pay the property taxes, gas, utilities and food. There was not any extra money for luxuries such as vacations, nice clothes, repairing fences or getting my hair done. I didn't even have health insurance. On paper I was a millionaire but in reality I was dead broke.

I was spiraling downward. If I didn't take action soon, I would stand to lose everything I had managed to keep after Brannon's death. Except for Matt, I felt isolated and depressed. I had to change my circumstances. I simply had to. Falling into the bed, Baby spooned me. My dreams were dreary, cloudy snippets of Brannon admonishing me; sleep was no comfort to me. Baby nestled his muzzle next to my neck, effectively taking away my pillow. His steady snorts of deep, contented slumber finally persuaded my whirling mind to push deeper until a numbing sleep claimed me.

12

On Monday morning I made an appointment with Shaneika's secretary. I put on a thick dose of mascara and dressed in an expensive but tightly fitted dress. I was going to have to lose weight, but like Scarlett, I'd think about that later. With resigned determination, I lifted a painting off my concrete wall, and wrapping it in an old comforter, placed it carefully in the back of my van. The traffic was awful as usual downtown, but I was able to find a parking space near the remodeled nineteenth-century bank building where her office was located. I was only a few minutes late for my appointment, but Miss Shaneika made me wait for twenty more. She could be petty like Matt. I doubted whether either one would ever tell me if I had spinach in my teeth.

Finally, I was let into a well-appointed nineteenth-century corner office with a restored mosaic floor that contained detailed Mason symbols. The room had glorious views of both Main and Short streets with their quaint buildings buffered by the old courthouse and glass skyscrapers. The furniture was mahogany, massive and expensive. Shaneika's desk had stacks of files on it as well as a silver-framed picture of a handsome young man smiling. I assumed he was her boyfriend. There were oil paintings of Kentucky Derby winners such as Aristides, Ben Brush and War Admiral on the walls.

Also hanging was a Confederate officer's sword, a tintype of African-American women on wash day at Camp Nelson and several letters, one of which was from Abraham Lincoln congratulating his brother-in-law, George Rogers Clark Todd, upon his graduation as a doctor from Transylvania University.

Leaning in closer to look at the Lincoln signature, I said, "I didn't know you were a Civil War buff."

"I'm not. Those are family heirlooms."

I shot a quick look at Shaneika.

Shaneika was wearing a beige Chanel suit with black piping. As far as I could tell, it was the real thing. It looked vintage. I wondered if it was a family heirloom too.

She spied the painting in my hands. "What's that?" she asked curiously.

I turned the painting over.

Shaneika gasped. "It's an Ellis Wilson!"

I smiled. "I noticed when you came to the farm that you seemed to be interested in the horses. I thought you might like this."

She clasped her well-manicured hands on the desk. "What's the catch?"

"As you know, I've no money to speak of." She started to interrupt, but I held up my hand. "I'm cash poor. I want to give this painting to you as a retainer. I am sure if you have it appraised, you will find it worth more than enough to compensate for your services."

"I don't get it. Your problems are over. Your bill has been paid. I told you that I owed your daughter a favor. Why do you need to keep me on retainer?"

"Because it is not over. I think Pidgeon's death was murder and I was set up. I'm going to find out who did it and why."

"You are asking for trouble. Let this thing go. Get on with your life."

"That's what everyone keeps telling me. How can I get on with my life with this thing always hanging over my head like Damocles' sword? I can't. Will you accept the painting as payment for being on retainer?"

She looked lovingly at the painting. "I never knew he painted horses."

"He was from Kentucky, after all."

She strode over to the painting and caressed the carved wooden frame. "Where did you get it?"

"I found it in a flea market and bought it for seventy-five dollars."

"Lucky bitch," Shaneika said, appraising me with a newfound respect.

"There's another matter. I wish to sell ten acres of my property for two hundred thousand dollars. I will not negotiate the price. I want you to find me a buyer and handle all the details. Of course, I don't have to tell you that I want this on the QT. Here's a sketch of the parcel I am selling."

Shaneika took the drawing that I had crudely drawn on notepaper and looked at it with interest. "This is not good enough. A surveyor is going to have to come out there. I'll arrange for one. Is water available?"

"Yes, there is a city water pump installed and a small

stream goes through. However, the stream dries up in the late summer for about a month, but the pump is in good working condition. There is also road frontage and the pasture is good for livestock."

"Two hundred thousand dollars is a bit steep, even for your property."

"God is not making any more Bluegrass."

"Any buildings on the property?"

"Just a run-down pony shed."

"If I remember correctly, this parcel is still in good fescue."

"I use the hay for my animals, so I've kept it up."

"You have a tractor?" asked Shaneika, sitting down and making notes on a legal pad.

"It runs, but it is kept together with a piece of baling wire and a prayer. Anyone nearby can be hired to mow the pasture."

"Okay, I will accept the painting after it has been appraised."

"That must come out of your retainer. I can't afford the cost of an appraisal."

"Why are you selling? I know you don't have any outstanding debt."

"My business – and quit checking up on me."

"Land and water are the two most precious things in the Bluegrass. People are stupid to sell. They can never buy back such prized land again. Once you sell out, you're out for good."

I held firm and said nothing. I knew it was a sacrifice, but I had no choice.

Shaneika gave me a hard look. Finally, she shrugged. "Okay, I'll take care of it." She called in her secretary and instructed her to prepare an invoice describing the painting. Then she stood. "I'll get back to you."

After my dismissal, I waited in the reception area while her assistant worked on a letter describing the painting. She popped her gum as she typed away. Handing me the finished letter and a receipt, she sent me on my way without a further glance.

I hurried home as I once again had garbage duty. As before, I dropped the Pidgeons' trash on the floor of the shed. I went through it quickly until I turned over a wet piece of paper encrusted with tomato seeds. The letter was confirming that a check of $750,000 had been sent to Tellie's current address. "Thank you, Jesus," I muttered, drying the paper with my shirt. At long last, my sifting through Tellie's garbage had produced results. I thought three-quarters of a million dollars was a good motive for murder. People had been killed for a lot less.

I suddenly felt energized, returning to my office at the house. I was meticulous when it came to records. I found my phone bills and began searching for Pidgeon's number after checking it in the local beekeeping association's list of beekeeper's numbers, which are given to members. Richard's number was indeed listed on my bill. The call was made in late August, just days before Richard's death. *Well, I'll be!*

13

Matt came home only to find me in the kitchen making a shrimp grits casserole. I was dressed in good clothes and my hair was brushed for once. "Hey Josiah, what's for dinner?"

I pushed him away from the steaming plate. "I am going to visit a sick friend, and taking this with me. I'm sorry, but I am going to miss movie night. Just can't be helped."

He looked disappointed. Every week for several years, Matt and I watched an old movie together.

"Look in the fridge for something to eat," I said. "Besides, I thought you said I couldn't cook."

"Just teasing you, Babe. You're a great cook." Matt brightened. "The mutt and I will take a swim first, then I'll make dinner."

"Clean up when you're finished," I requested as I headed out the door. "Oh, by the way the heater . . . "

"What?"

"Nothing. Have a good swim."

Matt grunted. His head was already stuck in my fridge. He wasn't paying any attention to me.

Abigail Keam

I opened and shut the front door, hiding in the foyer. Matt headed for the pool. Thinking that I was gone, I knew Matt would strip and jump into the deep end of the pool. I stood at the front door waiting.

Splash.

"Oh gawwd! Damn, it's cold!" I heard Matt yell.

Revenge is one of life's little pleasures. I couldn't help but smile. I headed for my van.

Forty minutes later, I pulled up in front of Tellie Pidgeon's house. Instead of heading for her front door, I knocked on her neighbor's. A few minutes later, an elderly man cautiously opened it with hands gnarled with arthritis.

"Excuse me for bothering you but I've come to see Tellie Pidgeon, but no one seems to be at home. I don't want to leave this casserole dish on the front porch. Dogs, you know, might get in it." I waited for a response.

"Well, no one is home. Mrs. Pidgeon works second shift and won't be home until midnight."

"Oh dear," I moaned. "What am I going to do with my casserole?" I looked point-blank at the man.

He cleared his throat. "I suppose I could take it."

"That would be great."

He reached for it, but I held on to the casserole. "You know, this is awfully hot. Just show me where to put it." I gave him my biggest smile.

Mr. Haggard – that was his name – showed me into the kitchen where I asked for a drink of water because I was "so parched." He obliged and invited me to sit at the kitchen table. I guess he was a widower, as I did not see a Mrs. Haggard or a woman's handiwork about the house.

"Isn't it awful about Mr. Pidgeon?" I inquired.

Mr. Haggard didn't respond.

"Did you know him very well?"

"Well enough."

My plan was not going to work if this old codger didn't open up. "How is Miss Tellie holding up?"

Mr. Haggard snorted. "I think she's doing better than average."

"Why is that?"

Mr. Haggard didn't respond.

This was hard work. What was it going to take to get him to spill his guts? "My name is Mrs. Reynolds and I worked with Richard at the Farmers' Market." I leaned forward and whispered in a confidential voice. "I don't like to speak ill of the dead, but some of his colleagues had problems with Richard. Didn't like his attitude."

Mr. Haggard seemed to warm up to this information. "Like he was uppity?"

"Yes," I nodded. "Hard to get along with. But I bet he was a good neighbor."

"The worst!" confided Mr. Haggard, who handed me a beer, forgetting that I had requested water.

I accepted even though I don't like beer. "Really?"

He pulled a padded chair out from a battered red aluminum kitchenette set and slowly bent into it. His wrinkled neck had a slight rash, which was probably poison ivy. "He was always complaining about my yard, said my tree limbs hung over his property and left leaves. He actually wanted me to cut down a hundred-year-old hickory tree because of the fall leaves," said Mr. Haggard. "Well, I'd rather cut off my right arm than do that. It's a sin to cut down a good tree, my way of thinking."

"What happened?"

"I paid for someone to rake the leaves up in his yard."

"No! I can't believe that."

"It's true." Mr. Haggard shook his head in disgust. "You know that man actually measured his grass?"

"Huh?" I was trying hard to picture that.

"Yep. That crazy hoss would mow his yard, and then get out a tape and measure the grass in the northwest corner. Then he would measure how tall the grass was in the southeastern part."

"Mr. Haggard, I think this is a tall tale," I said smiling.

The old man held up his hand. "Lord strike me down dead if I'm not telling you the awful truth. The man was just a plain nut. He used to drive my late missus to tears with his complaints about hanging her wash in the backyard. Said she had to move her clothesline, as he didn't like the wind blowing our clothes over the fence line of his property. He was always complaining about this or that . . . and poor Mrs. Pidgeon."

I leaned towards Mr. Haggard. "Yes?"

"Well," he took a swig of his beer, "let's just say she always had bruises on her arms."

BINGO! "You don't think he hit her, do you?"

"I never actually saw him do anything, but she had a lot of bruises. I don't think any woman can be that clumsy."

I stayed with Mr. Haggard for another twenty minutes before I found the way to my car. I gave him the grits, telling him that it would ruin before Tellie got home. I would make her another one. He seemed grateful at having a hot meal. He promised to return my dish to the Market.

On the way home, I left a message on Shaneika's answering machine that I wanted her to obtain copies of any emergency room reports on either Tellie or Taffy Pidgeon from the major hospitals in town.

She returned my call the next day and began complaining. "You know that is illegal. Medical records are confidential."

I laughed. "Quit being a drama queen. Take some of that money from my painting and bribe someone in the records department."

"Are you nuts?" she yelled into the phone. "I could lose my license."

"Just do it." I hung up before she could have the last word.

I didn't hear from Shaneika for over a week until a courier delivered a large envelope to my gate. It contained the Ellis Wilson appraisal. "Jumpin' Jehosophat!" I cried when seeing the painting's worth. Shaneika would be my lawyer until my death and then some.

Next, I pulled out four copies of emergency room medical reports for Tellie Pidgeon from several hospitals over a ten-year period. Cuts, bruises and a hairline fracture gave me what I needed. Each time, she said that she had been in a minor car accident or a mishap at home. Also included were Tellie's college records, work records and current financial status, which had been dire until she received Richard's life insurance check. It had been deposited but then she had had a cashier's check made out to her for $600,000. That was odd. All creditors had been paid except for the mortgage on the house, which was in the early stages of foreclosure. Strange, I thought. Why didn't she pay the house off? That would have been the first thing I would do.

Even some of Richard's medical records were included. It seemed that he had a weak heart and was being treated for high blood pressure, high cholesterol and OCD thrown in for good measure.

I laid Tellie's medical files, the insurance letter, college records, work records on my Nakashima table and began making notes on my yellow legal pad. Tellie had two motives – revenge and money. From her college transcripts, she had majored in pre-med and then dropped out. Her IQ was high.

Logically, a sleuth should always start looking at the person who has a possible motive closest to the victim and then move outward. Tellie was capable of planning an intricate murder. Where was she on the morning of Richard's death? I had motive but I needed to break her alibi. But then Agnes might have done it. If she still loved Richard, maybe she finally snapped because she couldn't have him. Or maybe there was some psycho killer roaming the countryside picking off beekeepers.

I then reviewed everything I had about Richard. All information led to a man who was angry, frustrated and in declining health. He was a prime candidate for a major heart attack. Maybe Tellie didn't want the additional burden of a physically disabled husband. Or maybe Taffy had learned of the insurance policy, and decided that her father stood in the way of her mother and herself living well. No, that couldn't be. She had an alibi on the morning of his death, but so did Tellie. I'd bet my farm that one of them or both had something to do with Richard's death.

*

That night, my daughter called me. "Mother, what you're doing is going to boomerang on you."

"Shaneika ratted me out, huh," I said. "Isn't my stuff with her supposed to be confidential?"

"Don't change the subject. What you are doing is irresponsible. You are going beyond badge work."

"Badges, badges? We ain't got no badges. We don't need no badges! I don't have to show you my stinkin' badge."

"The case is closed," responded my daughter tersely. Apparently, she did not think I was funny quoting from the *Treasure of the Sierra Madre.*

"There is no statute of limitation on murder. The police can reopen the case any time they like. Do you want someone to send the cops a little note causing them to reopen the case two years down the road? No, this needs to be settled now."

"What if your theory is wrong? Without substantial proof, Tellie can sue you for defamation of character if you go to the police with it."

"What if I'm not? I don't think I am, but I need to check on some things first. I won't do anything without talking with you."

"You can't involve me! I can't know anything. Understand? I am even going to cut off Shaneika."

"Yes." I knew she must not be connected in any form. It would ruin her.

There was silence on the phone. "All right, be careful," she said. As if she had to tell me.

14

Knowing that Agnes would never receive me at her office again, I tried a different ploy. For several mornings, I camped out on the immense marble reception porch of the Carnegie Center waiting for Agnes to park her big Cadillac that Officer Kelly had so nicely described for me. But I tired of standing against a massive pillar as the public skirted around me going into the building while giving me the once-over. So I retreated to my van. The first couple mornings, I had missed her as her car was already parked in her parking spot. Other mornings, she didn't show up at all. It seemed that she had a cushy job; she could come to work when she wanted. One morning, though, at 7:30, her Caddy rolled in. I slid down in my seat to prevent her from seeing me and calling the police.

Agnes parked some distance from me, so I silently got out, hoping to intercept her before she entered the Kentucky limestone building that housed her business.

"Good morning, Agnes."

She looked like a million bucks in her fur-trimmed suede coat, swinging a Kate Spade purse. Agnes recognized me immediately and reached for her cell phone.

"Before you call security," I added quickly, "you might want to know that I plan to tell the police that you omitted certain facts when you told them your story."

"Still drinking the blood of children?" Agnes said with quiet confidence. She unnerved me, but I was determined to have the last word with her. I had no idea why she was so hostile. A vampire – really!

"Look, we can do this in the cold or go somewhere warm."

"Get in my car and be quick about it," she commanded, looking down the tree-lined street.

She unlocked her car, and I slid into the passenger side. It had been a long time since I had been in a luxury car that had all the bells and whistles. I sank into the creamy champagne leather seat.

"What do you want?"

"One thing about being an academician is that one knows how to do research," I said reaching into my pocket, "like about your accident." I pulled out a copy of a newspaper article and handed it to her. "It seems that you lied to me, Agnes. There was, indeed, a car accident in which you and Richard were injured, but there was no other third party. You were the drunk driver."

Before she could respond, I produced a copy of her divorce decree. "And it wasn't you who wanted the divorce, it was Richard who wanted out – who told you to get lost. The only thing you told me that was true is that you loved him, which I believe you still do. It must have galled you that Richard went on with his life, married again and had a child."

Agnes was quiet. She started the car.

Not knowing what she was up to, I pulled my taser from

my pocket. "Don't try anything funny," I said.

"You sound like a cheap detective novel," she quipped. "Relax. We are just going around the block while talking. I don't really want to be seen sitting here talking to you." She settled back in the luxurious captain's chair and pulled out into the traffic. "I told you many truths. The accident did aggravate Richard's condition. It made him unbearable to live with. He began hitting me. One day, I hit back. Thought I had killed him. I never loved anyone but Richard, but I refused to let any man use me as a punching bag. What was there for us to do? Richard thought we should live apart before something awful happened. He loved me too. He was willing to let me go until he got better. He wanted the best for me."

"Yeah. He was a saint." I rolled my eyes. "So he divorced you."

"The plan was that when he had conquered his condition, we would remarry, but the thing is he didn't get better."

"And not only did he not come for you, but married a younger sweet thing. That must have been hard for you to take."

"Richard never really loved Tellie, but he wanted a child and . . . Tellie was convenient."

"You actually fell for that line of bull?"

"Tellie was what he needed."

"You mean someone compliant." An idea came to me. "Wait a minute! You and Richard never stopped seeing each other. You stayed in touch. You were always the real wife. Tellie was merely the woman who bore the child, cooked and cleaned for Richard, essentially a maid for him." I pointed a finger at Agnes. "But you were the one he loved. That is why you were going to make Richard the beneficiary of your will.

I bet he was always the beneficiary of your life insurance and pension as well."

"We had a standing date every week for the past twenty-seven years. We both got what we needed."

"Good Lord, you sound as though you're proud of this."

"I'm not ashamed of my love for Richard nor can you make me ashamed. I made the best of the cards dealt to me."

"How does Tellie play into all of this?"

"I lent him money to consult with the best doctors but no treatment ever helped him. It seemed like he was just hardwired to be a jerk but . . . other times, he was so sweet. We had been divorced for years when I told Richard I didn't think we were going to get married again. He would be wonderful for months and then without warning, he would be a monster and then go back to being wonderful again. I couldn't take it. Richard accepted that I loved him but I wouldn't live with him again. But he was still relatively young. He wanted a child, a family. Finally, he met Tellie. She was very passive and seemed to like being told what to do. She was what Richard needed."

"Did you ever meet her?"

"No, but I knew what she looked like."

"Did she know about your, uh, accommodation with Richard?"

A shrug.

"And your relationship with Richard was ongoing. You got the best from Richard while poor Tellie got the butt end of the stick."

Agnes said nothing, but concentrated on driving. It started to drizzle. She turned on the windshield wipers.

I tried another tact. "Do you think he beat Tellie?"

"I know that he sometimes slapped her, but not hard."

"He told you?"

"Yes, he had no secrets from me."

"On a regular basis?"

Another shrug. "It was none of my business what went on between them."

"You didn't call the police?"

"If Tellie wasn't going to call, who was I to interfere?" defended Agnes.

"He ever hit Taffy?"

"God no!" Agnes answered disgustedly.

"Are you sure?"

"Yes."

"Why?"

"Richard would have told me."

"Were you jealous of Tellie?" I continued pounding. I might never get another chance to discover the truth.

"Of Tellie, no. That she had a life with Richard – of that I was jealous."

"So, if you had been born a masochist, you would have stayed with him?"

"Yes. Some women are very much into being submissive. You need to ask Tellie about that lifestyle. I am just not put together that way."

"So it was Tellie's fault that she got hit?"

"If she is a masochist, then yes. She got what she wanted and needed."

"You are sitting there and actually telling me that women who are beaten by men are all masochists and want it. Do you know how weird you sound?"

"Do you know how stupid you are? I didn't ask to fall in love with a man whose habits I loathed. If you are one of those people who think a person can control whom they fall in love with, then you are stupid indeed. The heart has a will of its own. Besides there was more to Richard than what you saw. He was smart, funny and a good listener. Yes, he had faults, but you have no idea how hard he fought against his brutish nature. Sometimes he won. Sometimes he lost. I blame myself for it. If he hadn't been in that wreck, those traits might never have surfaced. And how in the hell am I to know what Tellie did or didn't like in their marriage? You don't know what went on between them. Maybe she loved the challenge."

"You should have moved on."

"Like you did?" sneered Agnes. "I did some checking of my own. Rumors around town say that you were having an affair with a Zac Efron look-alike gigolo and that's the reason your husband left you. He took up with a woman young enough to be his daughter and gave all his money to his little pregnant girlfriend."

I had been getting rather tired of Agnes' sanctimony, and now she had hit a hot button. "That brings me to what you told the police about needing to see Richard because you were making him your heir. What was that about? Why not just put his name on the will? You didn't need to talk with him to do that. What did you really talk to him about?"

Agnes sighed and lit a cigarette. She blew the smoke in my direction. "I wish you would just disappear. I really dislike you butting into my life."

"Tell me what I want to know and I'm just a memory." I snapped my fingers. "Gone, just like that."

"I have cancer."

I could hardly control my guffaw. "Christ Almighty, you're playing the cancer card."

Agnes tugged at her beautiful lustrous ink-black hair until it came off in a mass. In place of the wig were gray tufts of hair and wide patches of baldness.

"Removal of both my breasts, radiation, chemo, new age crap – you name it, I've tried it."

I should have been contrite. I should have been embarrassed. I should have been sympathetic. But I wasn't.

"Who is your heir now?"

"Taffy."

We had stopped at a red light. "Wow," I said. "It couldn't have happened to a more deserving person." I opened the car door and stepped out into the rain. Slamming the door shut, I began the walk back to my van, never looking back. I hoped I'd never have to see Agnes Bledsoe again. Talk about a bloodsucker.

15

I was checking on my bees in the early morning to make sure their water troughs were full. Like cows or horses, honeybees must be fed, watered and treated for diseases.

Today my job was making sure they had their winter medicine. I opened each hive and allowed the bees to gather at the top of the frames. Then I powdered them with powder sugar so that, when grooming, they would knock off verroa mites. While that occupied them, I placed peppermint candy canes in the hives, hoping that they would eat the canes allowing the peppermint oil to work on tracheal mites.

Since it was now nearly time for lunch, I made several sandwiches of thick roast beef with homemade potato salad. Putting everything in a handmade basket along with a big pitcher of martinis and a soda for me, I drove to see Larry Bingham, my bee mentor. He was the person who had helped me install my first package of honeybees. Without him, I never could have survived the travails of beekeeping. He was also president of the Lexington Beekeepers Association. If anyone had his ear to the ground, it was he, and I wanted information.

Larry was a retired FBI man who purchased 10 acres in Anderson County on which he kept hives and a garden. In the late summer, he puts a vegetable stand in front of his house. His customers are on the honor system, leaving money in a cigar box. Larry has made twenty-four thousand dollars this year so far.

I found Larry in his honey house putting honey jars in boxes. The Doors were blaring on the CD player. He sniffed the air. "What's buzzin', cousin?" He turned and smiled when he saw the basket. Walking over, he took the basket without even speaking to me.

"Hello to you too," I said laughing.

"Good to see you, Josiah. Shove your clutch down here." Larry pulled out a folding chair for me. Peeking in the basket, Larry's face flushed with pleasure. He handed me the soda and shook the pitcher. "This is going to hit the spot," he declared. "Bring any olives?"

I nodded, watching him pour a martini into a paper cup.

"Know what I had for lunch?"

I shook my head.

"Just a dried-out baloney sandwich, and I was lucky I got that. Brenda has me on some rotten diet. I had to sneak that crappy sandwich out of the house."

I glanced over at the back of the house. "I don't want to get in trouble here."

Larry waved at the house. "Don't get scared. The missus's gone into town. She will never know that you brought food to bribe me with."

I feigned offense. "Can't I just want to spend time with my good buddy?"

Larry loved puzzles, forties-era slang and late-sixties rock 'n' roll. Said that puzzles and riddles had always relaxed him even when it became his work, which was in intelligence during the Vietnam War. I would ask him to tell me about his spook operations for the government, but he never bit. Larry never engaged in war stories. Classified, I guess. Loving the Army, he would have made it his career, but life was going to go in a different direction. Wasn't it John Lennon who said that life is what happens when you are busy making other plans?

Larry had been on a two-day pass in Saigon when Charlie blew up the bar he was patronizing. It took six months before he was released from the hospital, and then the Army just let him go without fanfare. Larry thumbed his nose at the Army and joined the FBI. Since then, he had made it his business to notice things. He didn't stop just because he had retired. Now Larry fixed his watery blue eyes upon me.

"So, start beatin' up with the gums."

"Huh?'

"Spill it."

"Okay. Okay. I fess up. Larry, I might be in trouble. You know that Richard Pidgeon was found on my place dead."

Larry nodded his head while chewing. "Peeped it in the trees."

"Has there been much talk about that?"

"Talk, oh shoot-fire. It's all we yack about!" he replied, meaning the other beekeepers.

"What are the rest of the guys saying?"

"Different opinions about that. Some say Richard was messing with your hives, deserved what he got. Others just say that it was odd that he was on your property. Paper didn't divulge much except that he was found dead in a hive. Mystery is why would the bees sting a bee charmer? That's why gums are flapping. Something happened to rile up those bees against him; otherwise, Richard would never have gotten stung. Bees thought Richard was a solid sender."

I harrumphed.

Larry raised his hand to silence me. "I know you two had your differences, but Richard was a good beekeeper. Never saw a beeyard as clean as his. He loved honeybees, and his honey was as good as can be harvested. You can't take that away from him, sister."

I felt my face redden.

"Another thing," Larry said, reaching for the martini pitcher. "There were two cops here putting the squeeze on me about you and Richard."

"What did you tell them?"

"I played dumb. I don't dime to flatfoots. If it had been a Special Agent, well, then it might have been different, but I'm retired now. I don't need to play anymore," he said.

"Someone told them about the fight at the State Fair."

"It wasn't me that fingered you. You might want to look Tellie's way."

"Speaking of Tellie, have you seen her since this happened?"

"She has been awful quiet. I went over to her house twice, but no one answered the door. I knew she was at home because her Suburban was in the driveway. Seems like she wants nothing to do with beekeepers."

"Maybe it's you," I teased.

"Naw, dames love me. I had a condolence check for her from the Beekeepers Association and just put it in the mailbox."

"Cashed?"

"Not yet."

Larry removed his Red's ball cap and scratched his bald

head. "The thing for you to do is keep active, make sure you make the next bee meeting. If anyone asks about Richard, just say it's a mystery to you. No wisecracks. No bringing up the past. Keep it simple."

"So I look guilty?"

"You look anxious. I guess the police are turning the screws. They don't like unanswered questions. Neither do I."

"It's been officially ruled as a heart attack."

"Tell people that, but distance yourself from his death as much as possible."

"Do you think I had something to do with his death?"

"Naw, but someone sure-fire did. No bee would have stung Richard alive or dead without cause. Be careful. Watch your back, because someone gave those bees the meanies."

"I am just wondering. Why do you think that I had nothing to do with Richard's death?"

"You're no crab apple annie. You're too square. Dig? This was the work of a sneaky cat."

With that said, Brenda, Larry's wife, pulled into the driveway. Without blinking, Larry took the basket and martini pitcher, placing them under an empty box. He fished out some breath mints and took one. "Get me on the Ameche if you need something. I'll get the basket back to you at the next bee meeting," he said over his shoulder while going to greet his woman. I trotted along thinking about what he had said. I guess he knew something about sneaky people.

I ran errands and returned home to mow around the house. By dusk, I was feeling exhausted. I dressed in a ratty nightgown and climbed into bed early with Baby – not that I slept much, tossing, as my mind was restless again. I could see how people, when in a jam, panicked and ran. I was frightened. I was confused. For the first time in years, I wished Brannon were alive to tell me what to do. If things turned sour for me, I would have to start over in another town. At my age, I didn't think I had the strength to do so.

It was around 11:30 a.m. before I got up and fed Baby. It was time for the mail. I drove up the gravel driveway to the mailbox. I usually walked the distance, but it was misting. The mail consisted of the usual bills and invitations to church revivals.

An envelope with an old-fashioned typed address fell to the ground. I picked it up and opened it. Typed in big letters – "I KNOW WHAT YOU DID!"

I turned the envelope over. No return address. The person who sent the letter had used a manual typewriter. It was just like the letters sent to the police as described by Officer Kelly. Now the same person was sending hateful letters to me.

Many of the members of the Farmers' Market loathed technology and did not use computers. They still recorded their sales in handwritten ledgers. Could it be one of them?

When returning home, I put the letter on the dining room table. The next day, I wore latex gloves when getting the mail. Another letter. "MURDERESS!"

Carefully placing the letter in a baggie, I took it home. A magnifying glass showed that both letters were from the same typewriter as the D was missing its very top.

I suspected that a woman had sent it. Recalling an article I had read, women punctuate when writing threatening notes. A woman would use an exclamation mark to denote emotion. Men wouldn't bother. Also, it seemed to me that a man would use the word murder or murderer. Men always think in the male gender.

Matt came right over after I called him. He had been in

the cabana trysting with his new love, Franklin. I could smell sex on him. For a moment, the smell brought back a longing I had forgotten. Hastily, I turned my mind over to the letters.

"The canceled stamps say Richmond."

"Doesn't mean anything," I replied. "Someone could have been just passing through. It's only twenty miles away."

"On two consecutive days? I think the person either lives there or drives through Richmond for work."

"Could be right."

"Let's start with me taking these to the lab my firm uses. See if we can find anything on it."

"How much is that going to cost?" I was down to counting change for gas money.

"This is not the time to be penny-wise and pound foolish."

"Matt, no more than a thousand dollars. I mean it. I really can't afford that much."

"I'll do what I can. I'll also find out where Taffy works, and that is for free." He squeezed my shoulder. Matt then hurried back to his friend. He had forgotten the letters.

I sealed the letters in zip-lock bags. Walking to Matt's car, I put the bags on his dashboard. The lights of the cabana were turned off. I left in silence.

For a while, things were quiet. I went to work at the Market, making some good money. I didn't see anything of O'nan or Goetz. I started to relax, letting my guard down. Matt brought his new boyfriend home and invited me to dinner several nights. Grateful for company, I joined them at the cabana. It was lovely having the two of them cook while listening to their happy banter. Sometimes after dinner, they would take a quick swim while I curled up with Baby and a good book. I'd hear their squeals of play in the pool from my bedroom. Seeing their happiness had a positive effect on me.

I was never one for being resentful of other people's success. I wished them well.

Days later, the trees were in glorious fall foliage as I returned home from the Farmers' Market. Last spring's foals were prancing in well-mowed fields as I drove past horse farms on Tates Creek Road. A shy pileated woodpecker, winging through the sky, was a rare sight. I followed her flight until she was out of sight.

Turning into my rutted driveway, I stopped at the mailbox only to find another one of those dreadful letters, again from Richmond. I carefully opened the envelope, quickly reading it. I gasped. Feeling lightheaded, I struggled to open the van door. The slick paper slipped through my fingers, the world became a wall of darkness . . . and I slid into it.

16

I opened my eyes to see Matt looming above my face. His severe expression caused me to squeak like a mouse. "Where am I?" I croaked, struggling to sit up. My voice was hoarse.

"You're at the Medical Center. Josiah, you scared the bejeebies out of me. I thought you were . . ."

"Dead?"

"Yes, dead. You were lying in such an awkward position, half out of the van. It was still running." Matt ran his hand through his thick dark hair. "I was just plain scared."

I felt around my body to make sure all my fingers and toes were still intact. "Did I have a heart attack?"

"The doctor says it was asthma. It must have been a lightning-quick attack. I found an adrenaline shot in your purse, then put you in the van and drove like Old Scratch to get here."

I reached down and felt for my legs. My left thigh was very sore where Matt had jabbed me with the autoinjector.

"I didn't even know if you were breathing when they put you on the gurney. I am surprised I didn't run over anyone getting here."

"The letter?" I wanted to go back to sleep but struggled to stay focused. I was only half taking in what Matt was saying. Before drifting back to sleep, I heard Matt say something about staying the night for observation.

The next morning, I awoke in a semi-private room. I groaned, not because I felt ill, but because I had no health insurance. How was I going to pay for this hospital stay? Calling the nurse, I had her pull out the IV and got a gruff answer about when the doctor would be in.

While waiting, an elderly priest shuffled into my room after taking note of my room number. He patted my shoulder and began speaking in Latin. I could smell peppermint on his breath and Aqua Velva emanating from his thin papery skin. Recognizing that he was giving me the last rites, I interrupted, "Father. FATHER! I think there has been some mistake. I am just here for a short time."

The holy man looked at me sympathetically and responded, "Daughter, we are *all* here for a short time."

I stifled a laugh, letting him continue. I didn't have the heart to tell him I was Baptist. I made sure that I knew the name of his parish so I could send a note expressing my appreciation. After all, he did take time to try to make me feel better – somewhat.

When he shuffled out of my room, I called the nurse and had her show the priest to the correct patient. At that moment, I wished I were Catholic. I longed to confess. Just have someone to listen to my inane ramblings. I knew I had sinned three years ago and had not yet atoned for it. But I guess that's why God invented talk therapy for Protestants –

someone to listen to us verbally vomit. It was cheaper being Catholic, especially at a hundred eighty-five dollars a session.

After a hot shower, I dressed in clothes Matt had brought from the house and sat in the chair by the window, waiting for breakfast. Since I had paid for it, I was damn sure going to eat it.

Hearing a knock, I looked up to see Matt poke his head around the door.

"Don't you look better!" he said with relief. "You even washed your hair. So glad to see it. Now let's see if we can yank a comb through it."

I ignored his smart-ass remark about my hair. I remembered how he let me go into town only a few – how many weeks ago? It seemed like yesterday my hair was sticking straight up in full view of everyone.

"So what happened?"

Matt relished telling me about how he found me lying prostrate, how he and Franklin pulled me into the van and rushed me to the hospital. "Really, you weigh a ton. You have got to lose some weight, Babe."

"So it wasn't a heart attack?" I asked weakly.

"Nope. Just an old-fashion panic attack followed by an asthma attack – still could have been quite lethal."

"Did you find a letter nearby?"

"You mean this little old thing that said you killed your husband?" announced Franklin, who strolled through the door brandishing a soiled envelope in a baggie. "Sorry, but I was outside preparing for my grand entrance."

Franklin was as plain as Matt was beautiful. I guess he wasn't ugly, just non-descript looking. He was lean like Matt and had a face that – just was not interesting. His saving grace was an agile, playful mind that made him sexy.

Add his retro glasses, his dyed blond hair and his loud bow ties, Franklin screamed "flaming" but with style. I liked Franklin, but he made me feel clumsy. His mind worked so quickly. "Looks to me like some crabby old Mennonite typed this."

"Shut up, this is serious," snapped Matt.

"Let me see the letter," I demanded.

"I don't know about that," answered Matt, looking quizzically at Franklin. "I don't want a repeat of yesterday."

"What better place to have a relapse than in a hospital," I said, grabbing the letter out of Franklin's hand. I read it again.

"Want to confide in me?" asked Matt. It was plain that he was concerned that there was something to these letters. I had never discussed Brannon's death with him.

"Is this privileged?"

"Pay me a dollar." He looked at Franklin. "Get out."

"I'll just have to listen at the door," said Franklin on his way out.

"Hey, get me something to eat," I called after him. "I'm starving."

I handed the letter to Matt. It read, "THEE KILT THY HUSBAND TOO."

I gazed out the window. I didn't tell Matt about the priest's visit – how it had left a hard knot in my gut – but I needed to talk to someone. Matt was my best friend, but would he understand? I had to put my faith in our friendship, our common human experience.

It was hard to admit, but I have always felt guilty about Brannon. I had never explained the events leading up to Brannon's death to anyone, but now I needed to release the anguish.

"Brannon and I were in love for a long time but he fell out of love during the second decade of our marriage. For a while, he tried to put on a good face but I knew he was unhappy. We both wanted different things. Brannon wanted to live in a Tara."

Matt looked astonished.

"I kid you not. He hated the Butterfly. He would rather have lived in a palatial, antebellum plantation home with gleaming horses grazing in the paddocks, shuffling servants serving mint juleps, and Paul Sawyier prints on the walls. He wanted to be part of the old-money Kentucky aristocracy. I wanted to live in my contemporary house with most of the land reverting back to its natural state, a gravel road and wild animals roaming and a few run-down racehorses. He knew it would look odd if he wasn't living in what was his most awarded design so he put up with the bees stinging him, the peacocks pooping on his Mercedes, and the isolation. We had lots of money then. If it got too much for him, he would take a trip. I thought nothing of it – that was the way most marriages were after years of living together.

"It was five years, almost six years ago now, at a faculty Christmas party at the Art Museum that he met her."

"The name that can't be spoken?" asked Matt.

"Yes. In fact, I introduced them. Can you believe the irony of that?" I laughed bitterly. "She was a rich alumnus, divorced and bored. She had money, racehorses and a blueblood family name that went back generations – everything Brannon coveted. After several cocktails, they discovered they had many things in common – same type of art values, life values, money values. What can I say – they just clicked. Looking back, I would say the affair started that very night. Brannon was smitten. Two months later, he

116

moved out. A month after that, he wanted a divorce. I told him he could have the divorce if I could have everything else. I was going to bleed him dry." I paused, catching my breath. "He was just as hateful to me. This was not going to be a friendly divorce. The back and forth went on for several years with us both shelling out a fortune to lawyers.

"Finally, Brannon came to the house pleading with me to agree to a settlement. She was pregnant. He needed our life together over so he could marry her before the baby was born. I should have noticed that he was pale and rather thin at the time, but I was angry and distracted with his proposal. I just couldn't accept that our marriage had failed.

"I refused him. He left in a huff. Two hours later, I got a call that he was in the ER and had suffered a heart attack. When I got there, he had been moved to ICU. I commandeered the doctor who said that they were waiting for him to stabilize before they operated. He felt Brannon was too weak at the time.

"Then she showed up. There was lots of yelling and accusations. I wouldn't let her in his room. I was still Brannon's legal wife and had the hospital call security to have her removed. Even though I heard Brannon mumble her name, I wouldn't let her see him. He died later that night. I can't help but think that if I had let her see Brannon, he might have had the will to fight." I began to cry, dabbing my eyes with the bed sheet.

"It gets tackier: the reading of the will. I got his life insurance policy, an oversight on his part, I'm sure, while she got all the rest of his assets. I got nothing else. He didn't even leave anything to our daughter. Luckily, the farm was in my name only, an anniversary present to me, or she would have had half of that too. If I had gotten the full interest in his architecture firm, his paintings, bank accounts, retirement funds, I would be filthy rich. As it was, after I paid off the mortgage on the farm, I was broke and she was richer than ever."

"Did she have the baby?"

"His name is Brannon Reynolds III." I laughed. "She tells everyone that she is Brannon's widow, but his cremated ashes are in a cardboard box in my closet. Yeah, I had to pay for his cremation."

Matt handed me a tissue box. "Did I kill my husband? Perhaps the strain of our bickering added to the overall stress of the situation. But in some ways, I died just a little too, so I guess we are both even."

"I had no idea, Josiah. You never spoke of Brannon. I thought the two of you just went your separate ways. You never have let on how financially difficult it has been for you."

"I say that you have nothing to be sorry for," exclaimed Franklin as he burst into the room clutching his laptop. "What a soap opera! GAWD, could it get any worse for you? Having to lie to people about your circumstances – that you are one of the down and out poor. No wonder you kept it under wraps. Why, no one would take your calls if they knew you were one of the unwashed . . ."

"I thought I told you get to get me some food," I cut in.

Franklin plopped down on the bed. "I know how you feel, Josiah. If Matthew did something like that to me, I would be devastated. I mean, cheating is one thing, but not even leaving you a kopeck – that's a crime!" He pointed his tapered finger directly at Matt. "I would have done everything to keep him from making himself a fool over some shameless hussy."

"Is that what you call it?" retorted Matt.

"My Cherry Valance to your Matthew Garth," Franklin quipped, referring to Howard Hawk's *Red River*.

I looked accusingly at Matt. "You taught him the movie game?"

Matt grinned sheepishly.

"You are not thinking correctly," continued Franklin.

Both Matt and I looked cluelessly at each other.

"Look, someone is trying to spook you, Josiah, may I be so familiar. Mrs. Reynolds is just too formal after seeing you in your old lady undies. Sorry, but your shift had pulled up, let's not talk about how embarrassing that was to see. I thought I was going to go blind."

He turned to Matt, who stared furiously back at him. "Well, I did," Franklin said. "Who want to see an old lady catcher's mitt?" He continued, "Instead of spending a fortune on lab tests and lawyers, just use the Internet. Everyone spills their most personal affairs on the web."

I had no idea where Franklin was going with this diatribe. I was still wondering if I had had clean underwear without holes on when they found me.

"First of all, the language is just over the top. Who uses thee as you anymore? Comes across as very theatrical. Know anybody that speaks this way, maybe some old Amish lover you're not telling us about?"

I shook my head.

"While you were at the hospital with your husband, did any of the nurses, staff or doctors disapprove of your treatment of your husband?" asked Franklin.

"Not that I know of. Everyone was professional and courteous." I thought for a moment. "Golly, Franklin, I'm only fifty. You make me sound like I'm decomposing. Matt, do I really look that bad?"

"Josiah, stay focused. Okay?"

"Oh my God! My body really does disgust you," I said with my voice raised.

"Josiah," said Matt exasperated. "I think you are gorgeous for someone your age."

"*My age!*"

"Let's get back to the subject at hand," commanded Franklin. "I bet everyone was listening and someone on the staff disapproved. There are no secrets kept from the people who empty the bedpans. It may have looked like you were a harpy trying to keep this man's true love away. Do you remember any names?"

"No," I answered sullenly.

"That's okay," said Franklin, ignoring the storm clouds gathering in my eyes. He began typing. "I would bet that either Tellie or Taffy has a Facebook page. What we can do is see if any of their Facebook friends worked at the hospital during the time your husband was admitted. That person could have told Tellie or Taffy about your fight with the mistress." He fiddled with the laptop. "Tellie doesn't have a page but Taffy does. Let's see who her friends are."

He typed some more while whistling. "Okay, here is a list of friends. Let me know if any of the names seem familiar – or, better yet, look at their pictures." He placed the laptop on my lap.

"Don't you have to be accepted as a friend first before you can have access to her page?" quizzed Matt.

"Not if she hasn't put that on her privacy setter," said Franklin. "She's letting everyone have access to her page."

Matt looked over Franklin's shoulder. "It says right here on Taffy's profile that she works in the tourist industry in Berea. She must go through Richmond to get to work."

I scrolled down several dozen pictures trying to ignore the incendiary comments on her page about her father's death. My name was mentioned several times. Great. Finally I came to a woman who seemed familiar. I pointed her out to Franklin.

"See – all you needed was a computer. Not a detective." Franklin took his computer back and typed in some more. He looked up triumphantly. "It seems a Nancy Wasser is a retired ICU nurse from the Medical Center. You now have your link and can reasonably conclude that Taffy sent those letters." He punched in some letters. "I'm going to email her that I know Miss Josiah and that I think her honey tastes awful. Let's see what she says in return."

"No way," said Matt. "Unethical. That might be considered entrapment."

"Horse poo! I will do it myself using another name and my other email address."

"If this backfires, I had no knowledge of it – got it?" I said.

"Ditto," said Matt.

Franklin smiled. "Quote from *Ghost?*

Matt might be right about Taffy. We knew the connection and the manner of the letters. But why would Taffy use such archaic language? Thee and kilt was old mountain language, not in her frame of reference. And why send the letters to me?

Matt started to say something but my doctor came into the room. Twenty minutes later, I was wheeled to Matt's waiting car. I felt ugly, fat and repulsive, but I was on my way home. Those boys should volunteer at a hospice. There'd be laughs for all, including the corpses.

17

During the next several days, I stayed close to home. Matt and Franklin both made it a point to be at the farm before dark, taking over responsibility for its security and feeding of the animals. I think we were all a little spooked and needed life to assume an aura of calm and routine. Normal and boring sounded pretty good.

It also gave me the time to sew my costume for the annual Cherokee Stump Harvest Ball, which was the farmers' largest fundraiser. Matt was to be my escort. He was going as Prince Philip and I as Maleficent, one of my favorite Disney characters from childhood, which was not particularly healthy for an eight-year-old. It should have given my mother pause for her child to be pricking her doll's hands with a needle and shouting, "Touch the spindle. *Touch it, I say!!!*"

Sleeping Beauty was so passive, I was yawning even more than she was. Maleficent was a naughty fairy, who dressed in a truly magnificent purple and black gown with matching headpiece and a fantastic staff, making a real fashion statement to my eight-year-old mind. She suited me perfectly as I felt edgy and discordant, but I planned to have a good time with Matt, who happened to be an excellent dancer.

Franklin had already outfitted Matt with tights and a red cape. Matt made Franklin throw away the huge rhinestone codpiece he had glued together, saying he wouldn't be caught dead in it. Matt topped the costume off by confiscating my great grandfather's Civil War sword as the Sword of Truth.

On the night of the dance, Franklin showed up as giddy as a helicopter mom on prom night. He proceeded to help me into my costume, do my makeup, help don the headgear and then take pictures of both Matt and myself standing in the hallway holding hands. The only thing missing was a corsage.

Baby growled as we were leaving and snapped at the back of my dress. Franklin reprimanded him by saying, "Bad Baby. Bad Baby. Be good or I'll have to discipline you."

Matt grinned. "Nobody puts Baby in a corner."

Franklin groaned. "*Dirty Dancing.* Take care now, kids," he said waving goodbye.

I knew when coming home, Franklin and Baby would be happily ensconced in my bed while I would have to make do with the guest bedroom. Matt would bed down on the couch or sleep in the cabana.

Matt drove my ten-year-old Mercedes to Spindletop Hall, a classically styled mansion built with money from the Salt Dome oil field in Beaumont, Texas. It was so named, as it resembled a spindle top. Miles Frank Yount had acquired the leases on supposedly tapped-out plots and drilled deeper until he hit a second vein of oil in 1925. This was the origin of the great Spindletop fortune. Too bad old Miles died at the age of fifty-three. He didn't have much time to enjoy his good luck.

Yount's widow, Pansy, along with her grief, moved to

Kentucky to take part in the American Saddlebred industry. To claim her place among the gentry, Pansy built Spindletop Hall, a mansion that stood out among mansions in Lexington.

The house had 40 rooms including 14 bathrooms, which covered an area of 45,000 square feet. All pipes inside and outside were made of copper, as were 102 window screens. There were seventeen houses for servants, eighteen barns, one tennis court and one swimming pool, which sat on 1,066 acres of rich Bluegrass land. Pansy also had the largest Jersey cattle herd in the United States.

But things did not turn out well for Mrs. Yount. The Kentucky Blue Bloods did not accept Pansy or her newly acquired third husband, Mr. Grant, as the Texans were considered "new money." Our homegrown aristocracy can be very cruel.

The house was sold in 1959 to the University of Kentucky for less than its original building cost of a million dollars in 1935, and the locals have jealously guarded it ever since. Brannon thought it one of the most beautiful private residences he had ever seen.

In 1962, it became a private club for UK and hosted a variety of functions. One of the farmers, also a UK staff member, reserved Spindletop Hall for the farmers' annual Cherokee Stump Harvest Ball.

The grand hall was decorated with pumpkins and its curved double staircase encased with blinking lights and glittering fall leaves. The band played a mixture of rockabilly and swing music, and everyone was decked out in spectacular costumes – a great many of them dressed in authentic-looking Civil War garb. Away from public glare, the farmers could just be themselves, dancing the Cherokee Stomp or old-school jitterbug. There would be much drinking, eating, carousing and gossiping before the night ended. Maybe a little bottom-pinching here and there. Of course, that would occur after the church-going farmers had left.

After stuffing ourselves with Southern delicacies like country ham, corn pudding, cheese grits and sweet potato casserole from the heavily laden buffet table, Matt and I took to the dance floor, joining others doing the American Bandstand version of the jitterbug. In fact, most of the dancers were old enough to actually remember Dick Clark hosting his show from Philadelphia. I taught Matt steps that were simpler than the ones he had learned in dance school.

Matt was a wonderful dancer who made any partner look good. I noticed women eyeing him with open admiration while some of the men glanced at him furtively. I was proud of Matt's stunning good looks. I like beautiful things and he was beautiful.

"Oh, Matt," I cooed wistfully, "if only you were straight."

"Oh Josiah, if only you were a man," replied Matt as he twirled me around the room.

I was exhausted after the seventh dance. Matt sat me down at our table and fished out my albuterol spray as I had started to wheeze. He left to get some coffee, only to come back with a soda, which he plunked on the table.

"Taffy is here," he said, pushing the bottle with the tip of his finger towards me. I grabbed the green bottle and took a big gulp. "I'm going to ask you not to make a scene."

"I have a great big medical bill due to Taffy," I replied, scanning the crowded room.

"You have no proof that she sent those letters – just a hunch."

"Then this is a perfect occasion for getting some."

125

"Josiah, I have just started practicing law," Matt said softly. "I can't afford being associated with a catfight at Spindletop. Take it up with the courts and sue her."

Since Matt rarely made requests of me, I grudgingly acquiesced.

"Good, then I can tell you that bull dyke, Nancy Wasser, is with her," murmured Matt in my ear so bystanders could not hear him.

"I never thought Taffy was gay," I said.

"She may not be, but her friend definitely is. My gaydar went off the charts."

"And isn't Nancy a tad too old for her?"

Matt shrugged noncommittally. "What do people say about us?"

"But we're just friends."

"They don't know that. We think it's fun to make them think otherwise."

"Oh, how the plot thickens."

Matt excused himself to go to the men's room. I drifted outside onto the terrace to catch some fresh air. Several people were gathered in groups talking quietly. One of them was Taffy dressed as a scarecrow. When she saw my costume she smirked, whispering something to Nancy. I decided to say hello.

"Taffy, glad to see you getting out," I said smiling. "Is your mother here?"

"Nope, she's working."

"I understand that the medical examiner is releasing your father's body with the cause of death listed as a heart attack. I am sure that is a relief for both you and your mother." I had already forgotten my promise to Matt.

Taffy said nothing. I was hoping to bait her into revealing

something. "Is there going to be a service soon?"

"Yes. It will be in the paper," replied Taffy coldly, her scarecrow makeup making her eyes look abnormally large.

"I see. Who is your friend?"

I could see Taffy was becoming uncomfortable. It pleased me to see her squirm.

"This is Nancy Wasser."

"Nice to meet you," I replied.

Nancy stared at me, not uttering a word.

"Let's see, Nancy Wasser, Nancy Wasser. When my husband was ill, he had a nurse named Nancy Wasser. That was about three years ago. His name was Brannon Reynolds."

"I don't remember. I have had lots of patients."

"I could have sworn you were my husband's nurse. I guess that is why you are dressed as a nurse tonight, Ms. Wasser?"

"Are you suppose to be the devil or somethin'?" sneered Nancy.

"I am Maleficent from Sleeping Beauty."

"Doesn't she get killed by Prince Charming?" baited Taffy, looking at Nancy for approval.

"It's Prince Philip," I corrected. "But she does exact her revenge before she bites the bullet. I would keep that in mind."

Taffy immediately became sullen. "What do you mean by that?"

"I mean that when a particular type of person is pushed, they sometimes push back – hard. You know – the *Don't Tread On Me* motto."

Nancy snapped, "Lady, you sure got some sharp edges on you. A person is likely to prick themselves on you."

"Isn't that funny that you used the word prick . . ."

Sensing someone at my elbow, I turned around.

"Oh, darling, here you are," murmured Matt in my ear while pinching my elbow.

I stifled an "ooouch!"

Matt smiled at the ladies when he felt me flinch. "Good evening, Taffy. Please introduce me to your charming friend." Taffy introduced Nancy as Matt bowed and kissed Nancy's hand. "I adore your nurse and scarecrow outfits. How original."

I could tell Taffy and Nancy were wondering if they had just been insulted or praised. I was wondering myself.

"Showoff," I muttered under my breath.

Matt blocked my view of them. "Your drinks need freshening up. Allow me, please." He reached for both of their glasses, which they relinquished. "I hope that each one of you will honor me with a dance later this evening." Pulling at my sleeve, Matt said, "Come away, dear." Matt smiled back at the ladies.

Taffy beamed at Matt while her friend looked suspicious. Either way, Matt had two glasses in his hand as he steered me towards the kitchen. After talking with a waiter, Matt procured two baggies in which he deposited the glasses. "Get your stuff," he ordered. "We are leaving now."

I quickly grabbed my staff, purse and my grandfather's sword from our table. Hurriedly passing through the massive front doors, I hopped into the Mercedes, barely closing the door as Matt peeled away. I guess it had not occurred to her, but I now had Taffy's DNA and fingerprints. We made off like bandits.

Giddy with our success, we congratulated each other on the glass scam. We kissed, gave each other the high five and giggled like fools. We had taken Ironworks Pike, the back road to home, thinking that other guests including Taffy would take I-75. We were not paying the least bit of attention when we were suddenly hit from behind.

"What the . . . ?" yelled Matt, grabbing the steering wheel tighter. He glanced into the side mirror.

I turned around in my seat only to experience another jolt of the car hitting us. The car's brights were glaring so I couldn't see the type of car or driver. Matt was barely keeping my old Mercedes from careening off the road. Suddenly, the attacking car pulled into the opposite lane and sped up to become even with us.

"Watch it, Matt. They're going to run us off the road!" I cried.

Matt cursed at the other driver and slammed the brakes while the other car sped on. My car stopped in the middle of Ironworks Pike. Turning to each other, we both gave a collective sigh while watching the other car's tail lights disappear.

"Do you think that was Taffy?" I asked.

"Didn't you say that she drives a new Prius?"

"Yes."

"I really couldn't see who was driving or how many were in the car, but I don't think it was a Prius. Sat too high up," stated Matt

"They could have come in Nancy's car. I have no idea what she drives."

A car came around the bend from the other direction. Matt drove the Mercedes very slowly as he watched the car pass us.

"That's the car!" exclaimed Matt as he pushed down on the accelerator.

"The car that hit us? How can you tell?"

Matt didn't answer but concentrated on getting away from the "Christine" which had swerved around in the road and was now following us again at a fast clip. I was fumbling for my cell phone when the car slammed into us from behind again. I screamed. My purse spilled into the back seat. Frantically, I felt for my cell phone on the floor. Matt steered into the middle of the road, attempting to keep the other car from being even with us again. The car jolted us again from behind, rattling my teeth.

"Sweet Jesus," muttered Matt. We came to a wide spot in the road, which gave the other car room to become even with us.

I held on to the dashboard tightly as I knew what was coming. The car jammed into our side, causing us to run off the road, down a ditch, through a plank fence and into the horse pasture beyond. I caught glimpses of horses scattering out of our way. We finally came to a stop. Matt jumped out of the Mercedes yelling at me to get out. He ran over to my side, pulling me away from the Mercedes just as the car caught fire. The little explosion actually lifted me off the ground as I ran. Landing on my knees, I scrambled forward, half running, half crawling. I heard Matt panting behind me. Feeling I was far enough away, I turned to face the burning car.

"Matt, make sure no horses are around the car," I cried, searching the dark for a house or lighted barn. I didn't need to worry, as the mares and their foals had rushed to the other side of the pasture. But their screaming and neighing was disturbing and only added confusion to the situation. A light flickered on in a house at the edge of the field.

Within twenty minutes, a fire truck, three police cars, an ambulance and a very angry landowner's jeep surrounded my now smoldering Mercedes. I was getting lots of unwanted attention from policemen who were asking me to walk a straight line and to breathe into a tube. Anxious to keep Matt out of harm's way, I said I had been driving the car, as he was not listed on the insurance. When the police were finished with me, I sat in the back of the ambulance wrapped in a blanket, watching several half-dressed Mexicans herd the excited horses into another field.

The owner of the property was stomping before me, cussing a blue streak, which did not help the situation at all. I disliked being the verbal victim of an overly-Botoxed, big-boobed trophy wife who had probably never purchased a real piece of art in her life. She looked like the type who had a print of dogs playing poker in her study. I waited while she made threats of lawsuits and court proceedings until I asked the lady if she had good farm insurance. I pointed out that I was hurt on her land as the result of a crime. Lawsuits can work both ways, I reminded her. Exasperated, she walked off in a huff, stepping in some horse manure ruining her pretty house slippers. The paramedic, tending my cuts, chuckled.

The police finally acknowledged that we were not staggering drunk and took our statements independently. The car was towed off for the insurance adjuster. I was sure it would be totaled and the insurance company would issue a check for a pittance. I couldn't afford a new car, let alone another Mercedes. Another piece of my past life had just slipped away.

Muscles sore, costumes dirty and tattered, Matt and I were driven home by the police. We staggered into the house around four a.m. I made us both a drink. Rubbing my neck, I was grateful that I had a neck brace tucked in my bathroom closet. I was going to put it on before I went to bed.

"What a screwed-up night," commented Matt.

"My sentiments exactly."

"Someone was trying to kill us."

"It would seem so."

"Perhaps they will find the other car's paint on your Mercedes."

"Or I could track down Taffy's new hybrid and see if there are any scratch marks on it."

"Stay away from that loony. She's not all there. I'm sure she's the one who tried to kill us. Who else would even know we were on that particular road?" He cupped his head in his hands. "I just can't believe it."

"As you said before, we have a theory but no proof."

Matt moaned. "Ahh, the glasses."

For the first time in hours, I smiled. Holding up my purse, I dumped its contents onto the kitchen island. Large shards of glass fell onto the teak wood countertop.

"We may have more than a theory. I put the glasses in my purse. It's what saved them."

Matt picked up the shards with a paper towel, placing them in a new large bag. "Someone knows that you are still looking into Richard's death and is trying to stop you."

"That's why I don't want you to come around anymore, Matt. This thing is getting too close to you."

"But I live here. I am just getting the cabana where it is livable for winter."

"You need to stay in town – until this blows over."

Matt looked astonished. "Don't do this."

"You said yourself earlier tonight – you are just starting a new career. You have your whole life ahead of you. I don't want to tarnish your future with my problems."

"So I'm supposed to run at the first sign of trouble. I was in that car too. You don't think much of me, do you?"

"It is not that . . . it's that I want to protect you."

"I don't need your protection. I'm a grown man. It seems that you're the one needing protection."

"I'm older than you . . ."

"But you're not smarter than me nor wiser. If I turned my back now, I couldn't look at myself in the mirror. I'm seeing this through."

I shook my head. "I don't want you here. You're just in the way."

"Shut up, Josiah. You're really pissing me off. I need you to shut your mouth up now." Matt picked up his drink and went into my bedroom, where Franklin was probably awake listening. He closed the door silently.

I went to sleep in the guest bedroom. For some reason, I couldn't cry.

18

The next morning, I found a sullen Matt munching on cornflakes in the kitchen. Neither of us spoke as I made tea. I busied myself with reading yesterday's newspaper while each of us slurped, slurped, crunched, crunched in our fashion until Franklin, in a dazzling white shirt accented by a green bow tie with purple polka dots, swept into the kitchen.

Baby happily padded after him. Upon seeing me, he came over to be petted, trying to climb into my lap. I rubbed his floppy ears while he buried his soft muzzle in my crotch.

Franklin threw his arms around me in a dramatic gesture, saying, "Matt may be a boy to you, but last night he showed me what it means to be a man."

"Ooooh nasty, too much information," I said laughing as Matt flung some soggy cornflakes at Franklin's head.

"Okay, kiddies, kiss and make up. I am sure last night's fight was fueled by fear, the specter of death and an abundance of alcohol," coaxed Franklin. "Come on. Come on. Today's a new day. Matt, you'll need to handle the car insurance and police people, acting as Josiah's attorney.

Please don't bill her as she lets you live here rent free in her tacky little caretaker's shack." Franklin squeezed my arm. "I don't think you know this, dear, but Matt gave up his apartment in Lexington to be with you. You simply cannot throw him out now. Besides Josiah, darling, you are going with me this morning. We've a car to check out."

"Well, I've got my marching orders," said Matt, sliding off the barstool. He put his hand on my shoulder. I patted it affectionately. Neither of us spoke.

Franklin looked at us sympathetically. "It is a real shame that the two of you can't really hook up, but then . . . c'est la vie. Let's get crackin'."

Following me into my bedroom, Franklin rummaged through my closet, picking out the day's outfit. "I am tired of seeing you look like Marjorie Main." He threw a dress at me when I came out of the shower. "Here's something that doesn't look like a feed sack."

Ignoring the dress, I put on jeans, boots and a thin sweater. I brushed my hair and put it up with a clip. "Let's go," I said, walking out of the room.

"Middle-aged women should not wear jeans. It makes their already big butts look humongous," said Franklin, scrambling after me. We went in Franklin's Smart Car. Of course, Franklin loved his car and would not hear of any criticism. When not hanging on to the passenger strap for dear life, I checked out Franklin's music.

"Really, Franklin. ABBA?" I said with scorn.

He grabbed the CD out of my hand. "Everyone has a guilty pleasure, Miss Good Taste dressing like a charwoman."

"Okay, okay," I said as I continued to browse through his CD box. "Genevieve Waite's *Romance Is On The Rise* 1974." I looked at him in amazement. "You know who Genevieve Waite is?"

"Of course, doesn't everyone?"

"My hat is off to you, Franklin. Here I thought you were just a vacuous pretty boy for Matt. It seems like you have depth after all."

He smirked. "As if I'm pretty." He glanced in the rear view mirror. "Think so?"

"Do you think I'm pretty, Franklin?"

"Oh, God no."

"Then I don't think you're pretty either."

We both laughed as we raced the back roads. On the way, I called Officer Kelly on my cell phone and told him of last night's incident. He said he would look into it for me. I also told him about Nancy Wasser, asking him if he could check on her for me. He replied he would do what he could.

Then I called Shaneika, catching her for once and told her about last night's adventure. She had a friend in the city's Vehicle and Boat Tax Division. She promised to call me back when she found out some information. When I asked her how this information could be gotten on a Sunday, Shaneika told me to mind my own business. I wondered if she could work the internet or had someone on the inside. Regardless, fifteen minutes later, she called back with both Taffy's and Nancy's VIN and license plate numbers complete with model, year and make.

Franklin and I drove to Taffy's apartment, where we located her Prius in the parking lot but found no scratches or dents. Finding Taffy's car unlocked, Franklin quickly did a search. After all, she did not know of Franklin's existence and would not recognize him if she saw him rifling through her car. The car was clean except for a few Mars candy bar wrappers. Not wanting to give up, Franklin insisted we drive to Wasser's house.

Nancy Wasser lived on the other side of town, but we got there quickly for the churches had not let out yet. Wasser's house was a one-story red brick home in a low-income neighborhood. The street was lined with mature pin oak trees standing guard over tidy homes and velvet green lawns.

Franklin drove slowly by Wasser's house and spotted her car parked on the street directly in front of her home. He drove to the end of the corner, turned around and parked four doors away from Wasser's house.

"Stay here," he said while getting out with his camera. He looked both ways. No one was visible. Franklin was casually strolling up to the car when Taffy and Nancy exploded from the house.

I slumped down in my seat. I couldn't hear what they were saying, but Taffy seemed upset. Nancy grabbed Taffy's arm while trying to reason with her. Taffy pulled away brusquely. Franklin walked past them, continuing up the street until he disappeared around the corner. Enraged, Taffy yelled something crude and got into Nancy's car only to speed off. Nancy, looking distraught, tugged her robe about her and went back inside the house, slamming the door. She pulled the front curtains shut.

Several minutes later, Franklin, having circled the block, got back into the car. Without saying a word, he drove towards Matt's office. Once we were out of the neighborhood, he motioned for me to sit up.

"My, that was thrilling!" exclaimed Franklin. "Did you see how cool I was under the gun, so to speak?"

"What were they saying?"

"Taffy said something like 'you had no right. You're gonna get me in trouble.' Something like that."

"Could mean anything," I replied. I thought for a

moment. "See any dents in the car?"

"I didn't dare look. I was concentrating on keeping my breakfast down. I mean, how exciting. I can't wait to tell Matt everything."

"Do you think those two are an item?"

"I don't know, but it would seem that Miss Nancy wishes they were."

"It just seems strange, Franklin. I mean, I have always seen Taffy with serious boyfriends."

"Maybe she got tired of the same old, same old and wanted to walk on the wild side."

"Maybe," I said. I let Franklin off at Matt's office and drove Franklin's car home. I knew Matt would be hauling Franklin back to the farm to eat an early dinner. We had learned little except that Taffy may or may not be having a lesbian affair. Who in the hell cared about that? Not me.

19

Later that afternoon, Matt and Franklin showed up looking for a hot meal. I was ready with chicken and dumplings, greens flavored with ham hock, skillet fried corn, chilled sliced tomatoes and biscuits slathered with my Black Locust honey – everything purchased from the Farmers' Market. We sat at the Nakashima table watching the sun drift behind the hills in Madison County, just across the river. Having overeaten, Matt unbuttoned his pants and rambled over to the couch. He was soon asleep, snoring with the Sunday paper lying on his chest.

I turned to Franklin. "You don't look very well, Franklin."

"What do you mean? I feel fine," he replied somewhat alarmed, touching his hand to his forehead.

"No, you don't," I insisted. "Your skin looks sweaty and gray. Let's go to the LETC and get you checked out."

A sudden realization dawned on Franklin. "No, after this morning, I have had enough. I just want to relax after this great meal."

Yanking Franklin from the chair, I said, "Life is a banquet and most poor suckers are starving to death!"

"Rosalind Russell in *Auntie Mame* and I won't go."

I got in Franklin's face. "Aren't you tired of working in a drab room cranking out software? Don't you want adventure? Don't you want to be like T.E. Lawrence or Richard Burton?"

"The actor?"

"No, the explorer of the Nile River. Come on, Franklin, Live, live, live! You need something to write memoirs about," I yammered as I pushed him out the door. I grabbed the keys to Franklin's Smart Car and off we went.

We had just pulled onto Tates Creek Road when Franklin's cell phone buzzed. I grabbed it from him, turned it off and threw it in the back seat.

"You're a hateful woman," said Franklin. "I bet that was Matt."

"I know it was Matt. What he doesn't know won't hurt him."

"Such a cliché."

"Life is a cliché from time to time. How old are you? Twenty-eight, twenty-nine. Just wait, Franklin. Life has got some surprises waiting for you, like lots and lots of clichés."

Franklin did not address me the rest of the trip, but used the time to perfect his moaning and stomach clutching. He inspected his grimaces in the rear-view mirror. Drama was my minor," he confided as I pulled into the LETC parking lot.

"Never would have figured you for a drama queen."

"Ha ha, very funny," said Franklin rolling his eyes.

"You're teasing, Franklin. I know you have a Bachelor of Science from UK."

"Well, actually, I have two degrees – one in computer science and the other in mathematics, but I love drama."

"No kidding."

I helped a trembling Franklin stumble into the LETC waiting room and up to the front desk. Luckily there were only a few people in the waiting room. To our relief, no one looked as though they had anything contagious. A clerk handed Franklin some forms to fill out. "Who is going to pay for this?" hissed Franklin in between obligatory moans.

"I will pay for whatever your insurance doesn't cover."

Franklin snorted. "Yeah, like you're Diamond Jim Brady. I'll never see a single sou out of you."

"Yes, you will. Just write down the information and let's get on with this."

I took the completed forms back to the front desk, but had a momentary lapse when trying to hand over the insurance card. It didn't seem to want to leave my fingers. The clerk began tugging the card to get it from me.

"Sorry," I mumbled. It had felt so good to hold a medical insurance card, something I hadn't had for several years. I could feel the clerk watching me as I took my place beside Franklin. I tried to look inconspicuous as I read *Field and Stream*.

Ten minutes later, we were inside an examining room. I explained that I was Franklin's older sister and that he was a mid-life baby, which explained the difference in our ages; and due to the painful labor our mother endured on his behalf, he was "not all there." Franklin started to complain loudly about abdominal pain.

The nurse noted all the symptoms on a little computer board, giving us the once-over before she left the room. I tried to look sympathetic. Franklin tried to look sick. We both probably looked like we were up to no good – which, of course, we were.

A friendly Asian doctor came in several minutes later, asked pertinent questions in a thick accent, examined Franklin, and ordered him to be whisked off to x-ray. A technician soon came for Franklin, explaining to us in slow enunciation where she was taking him. Apparently, the word had made the rounds that our parents had been first cousins. Franklin followed her, shuffling and complaining that he needed a wheelchair.

The nurse came back to straighten the room, but I suspected it was really to keep an eye on moi and keep me from ripping off the clinic's latex gloves, sterile cotton balls and outdated *O* magazines. I found this the perfect opportunity to ask about Tellie. "I have an acquaintance who works here," I said. "Her name is Tellie Pidgeon. Is she here today?"

Nurse Ratched suddenly warmed up to me. "She has had a death in her family and is not working her regular schedule."

"I knew her husband, Richard Pidegon. I thought if she were here, I would express my condolences."

The nurse looked at the computer board searching for my name, which I had given as Frances Farmer, the mentally unstable 30's movie actress. If they asked for ID, I was a dead duck. "There seems to have been some question about how Richard died."

"Oh really," I said feigning surprise.

The nurse looked up from her board. "Oh, nothing sinister. Apparently he keeled over in some woman's beehive, and Tellie wanted to find out whether he died from bee stings or from some other cause."

I shuddered. "Bees scare me. I just swell up like a puff ball when stung."

The nurse nodded in agreement. "I guess if he was killed by the bees, there will be a lawsuit."

Wonderful. "But she still comes into work?"

"On an irregular basis, until she can get a handle on all the paperwork you know, will, insurance, funeral arrangements."

"Sure. Tell her I said howdy."

"Will do," the nurse said, leaving the room.

I was left alone to peruse old copies of *Golf* and *Parenting* magazines, neither of which thrilled me. Why don't offices ever order *Vanity Fair* or *Vogue?* Forty-five minutes later, I was helping Franklin back into his car with a prescription to settle his supposedly bad case of indigestion.

"What did you find out?" I asked Franklin.

"I have no obstructions in my bowels."

I cast an irritated look at Franklin as I started the car.

"Oh you mean about Tellie's alibi buddy – Joyce Kramer. It would seem our Joyce Kramer recently came into some money and has taken six months off."

"Really?"

"Yep. Convenient, isn't it."

"Why is she taking six months off?" I asked.

"The excuse was that she has a sick child she wants to spend time with."

"Where did the money come from?"

"The nurse just said it was a surprise windfall."

"Maybe the windfall came from Tellie, who paid Joyce to lie and punch in Tellie's time card on the morning of Richard's death."

"How can that be done with the other employees about?"

"If it's a slow morning, employees could be running out for a quick breakfast or dozing in the back. Joyce could have said Tellie was in the bathroom if anyone inquired where she was. I think it would be easy to sneak out of a place like that. It's only twenty minutes to my place. Richard could have picked her up and then driven out to my house. Then Tellie would only need five to ten minutes to kill Richard," I surmised. "Richard is looking at the hives and she comes from behind and stabs him with the adrenaline pen. He has a heart attack and falls into the hive. Tellie drives the same car home."

"That's an awful lot of ifs," cautioned Franklin.

I was on a roll. "That has her missing just half an hour of work. It would have taken her forty minutes to drive to her house, but no one would be looking for her at that time. She can easily explain to the police that she was driving home from work when Richard was at my place." Franklin started to say something but I interrupted. "The ground was dry and the grass had been cut so no car tracks were noticeable." I smiled. "See, everything fits."

"Why don't you just ask Tellie? Confront her and see how she reacts," said Franklin.

"I'm trying to avoid having any kind of confrontation with the widow of the man who died on my property. That wouldn't serve me any good. Why would she tell me the truth, in any case? She would just call the police on me. I need to keep tabs on her and see if I can catch her in a slip-up without her knowing that I'm snooping around."

"Oh, I forgot to give this to you the other day. When you were at the ball with Matt, I did some more snooping on Facebook. I found out that Nancy Wasser likes to frequent The Racetrack."

"The Racetrack? Isn't that a strip joint?"

"Yep."

"I don't get it."

"You're so behind the times. If it is post-1999, you don't seem to keep up. I mean – have you bought any new clothes in this decade?"

"Franklin!"

"The new thing with girls is they go to strip joints and get lap dances."

"No way."

"Way."

I thought for a moment. I knew the manager at The Racetrack. I had met her at a church function. I bet if I explained the circumstances, she would help me. She seemed on the up and up. What could it hurt?

The next afternoon, I trotted over to see Goldie, who although the manager of a strip-club, was a very religious woman who attended one of the four hundred churches that dot the Bluegrass.

One time, an English tourist, buying from me at the Farmers' Market, questioned the number of churches. "There is a church on every corner!" she exclaimed. "I've never seen so many churches."

"Well ma'am, it is due to the fact that we are such great sinners. We sin Monday through Saturday and go ask the Lord for forgiveness on Sunday morning."

"Must be a lot of sin."

"Yes ma'am, among other hell-raising. We are not a quiet people. Remember most Lexingtonians have Scots/Irish blood."

"That explains it."

"Our love of religion can be traced back to the Second Great Awakening in 1801. The descendants of those twenty thousand people who attended the revival still maintain a strong influence on our culture. If you look in your tourist brochure, you can visit the actual site in Cane Ridge, not far from here."

"I noticed you said love of religion and not love of God."

"Ma'am, we Kentuckians may make illegal whiskey, bet on the ponies, shoot each other in blood feuds and run drugs up I-75, but we still love Jesus."

So it wasn't a contradiction to me when I walked into The Racetrack to meet a church-goin' woman. The Racetrack was a dimly lit, nondescript building. A burly man wearing a white shirt and orange sweat pants, who acted as both bouncer and bartender for the light afternoon crowd, greeted me. Music was playing softly, but a dancer was nowhere to be seen. Men and a few women sat quietly at separate tables drinking. I asked to see Goldie, who was nicknamed for the twenty gold bracelets she wore. Clever of her, huh?

The man motioned for me to take a seat at the bar while he made a call. I ordered a Bloody Mary. A few minutes later, a harried-looking woman with wild gray hair joined me at the bar. She was wearing a smart gray pants suit with a retro Pucci scarf. Goldie gave me a quick hug before asking for some coffee.

"I take it this is not a social visit," Goldie said looking quizzically at me.

"I was hoping you could help me with some information. I know you are busy and I don't want to take much of your time, but if you would give me ten minutes, I'll get out of your hair."

Goldie seemed interested. "Okay, shoot."

I quickly told her that I had been run off the road and nearly killed. I had two suspects in mind but I couldn't prove anything. I had reason to believe that one of the suspects frequented Goldie's place. Pulling out pictures of Taffy and

Nancy downloaded from Taffy's Facebook page, I pushed them towards Goldie.

She studied them intently. "Don't know them, but leave the pictures here. I'll show them to my girls and call you if anything turns up."

"Thank you." I pulled out a business card along with a hundred dollar bill. She took the card. "If something turns up, I would like some honey," requested Goldie. "I love honey with my oatmeal." Without saying goodbye, she returned to the bowels of the club.

The bartender, who had been listening, palmed the hundred dollars and returned to wiping down the bar with a dirty bar towel. I looked at him astonished as he turned his back on me. I left the bar, wishing I had my hundred dollars back.

That afternoon, I helped Matt repair the heater on the pool. He worried with some corroding wires while I told him about going to the strip joint. "I hope I hear from her," I said as Matt flashed a light into the pump box. After pulling out a carcass of a mouse and making repairs with duct tape, I forgot about the strip club and focused on the rotting guts of my pool. Over thirty years old, the pool's pipes and mechanics needed to be replaced. I went to bed depressed.

The Racetrack was a long shot but sometimes long shots come in. The next morning, Goldie called me. "Got something for you. Come around ten to talk to one of my girls."

"Ten a.m.?"

"Ten tonight," she chuckled.

"Oh, all right. Will be there."

Goldie hung up without another word. Apparently she didn't like to say goodbye. I wasn't sure whether to conclude this was rude or just plain cool.

My next assignment was to decide what to wear. My assortment of clothing had shrunk as my waistline expanded. Matt was right. I was not just Rubenesque but getting very fat. The stress of the past several months had turned me into a serious stress-eater and it didn't seem that it was going to abate soon. I chose a sports outfit. If I wasn't fit, I could at least look like I hadn't given up. I fidgeted with my lipstick and actually tried to groom my hair into something that looked styled. Having no real idea why I was nervous, I eventually put it down to the thought of being in a room full of drunken men lusting after young fresh things who showed their personal life for all to see. The idea of sex made me queasy. It dredged up deeply buried feelings that, if surfaced, would make me feel restless and angry. I had enough to deal with. I just hoped no one would make a rude comment about me being a porker.

I arrived a little after ten, explaining to the doorman that I had an appointment to see Goldie. While he looked skeptical, he made a call on the house phone. I stood out of the way while other patrons paid their cover charge to get in. The odors of alcohol, men's cologne with body odor and baby powder ran together. The waitresses wore jockey hats and satin low-cut blouses that tied around the waist accompanied by jodhpurs and knee-high riding boots. I thought they were sexier than the near naked women dancing on the stage. Finally, the door manager's phone rang. He listened and hung up. "Go to the last door on the left."

Nodding thanks, I pushed my way through a hothouse of men of all shapes and sizes looking for a good time. Someone cupped my ass as I made my way through. I didn't even look back. I just kept moving forward until I got to the hallway. Knocking on the last door, I got a faint response. Opening the door gingerly, I peeped in to find a spacious, professional and very clean office. It looked like it belonged to an accountant, which made the nearly nude woman sitting in a chair out of place. She had on a flimsy robe through which I could see every dimple, every curve underneath.

Sitting behind her desk, Goldie motioned me to sit down in a leather stuffed chair. "This is Daisy," introduced Goldie. "She says one of your girls came in last night throwing around a lot of cash. Daisy entertained her privately and overheard her talk on her cell phone."

I looked at Daisy, who sported a feathered blond haircut and a barbwire tattoo around one of her wrists. She had nice full breasts, one of which had a nipple ring. The sight of it made me wince. Goldie handed me Nancy's picture.

"You said this woman came in last night?"

"She came in right around eleven-thirty. Her name is Nancy. She sometimes comes in with another chick."

I held up Taffy's picture. "This girl?"

"Yeah, right, but usually without her. She's a lesbo. One of my regulars. Drinks a lot and then asks for private lap dances."

"Lap dances?"

"Yeah, sometimes five before she leaves."

"Isn't that expensive?"

"Yeah, but that's not my problem."

"Does dancing for women bother you?"

"No, I sometimes date women myself. So do many of the girls who work here."

"Of course. I'm sure Goldie has filled you in that someone ran me off the road the other day and nearly killed me – totaled my car. I think it was Nancy but I can't prove it.

Did she say anything that might help me?"

"She was talking to some bimbo on her cell. I think the other girl was leaving her, 'cause she started crying. She said stuff like, 'I know I shouldn't have done it, but that bitch made me so mad. The police will never make the connection.' Stuff like that."

"Sounds like she may be your girl," commented Goldie.

"Could be, or could be she was talking about a parking ticket. Anything else?"

Daisy shook her head. "Look – I've got a show coming up, so I gotta go. I wish I could help you more. Having someone hit my car and run off would make me really mad but that's all I heard. I hope you catch the creep who did it."

"Well, I appreciate it."

"On your way out, catch my act."

"Thanks. I might."

Daisy ran off to do her show while Goldie and I made small talk about people we both knew. Almost forgetting, I pulled out several jars of Wildflower Honey from my coat.

"Hey, you remembered," Goldie cried happily. She seized the bottles with gusto, locking them up in her desk. Looking at my startled expression, she replied, "If I don't, the girls will *borrow* them." She rose from her desk. My time was over.

As we were both walking out, I asked, "Hey Goldie, don't women date men anymore?"

"Honey, people don't date anymore. They hook up. We are both old dinosaurs. Gotta get used to the way the world is today."

Goldie escorted me out of her office pledging that she would call if she heard anything else. She gave me a goodbye bear hug. Plunging back onto the floor, I saw that Daisy was performing.

I don't understand pole dancing. I prefer the feather-fan strip-tease era with strippers like Gypsy Rose Lee and Sally Rand, but Daisy wasn't half bad. The men looking at her were seemingly in a trance. Once in a while, one would reach up and put money between her legs. Daisy had muscles like a vise-grip, never letting a dollar drop. I scooted my way to the door. Seeing me, Daisy winked and blew me a kiss. I stepped out into the cold air.

20

It was finally in the paper that a memorial service was scheduled for Richard. I could now have contact with Tellie with a good excuse. I would just go to pay my respects while hoping to find out stuff – what stuff I didn't know.

I donned a black dress I had worn when I was pregnant. I brushed my red hair into a tasteful French twist and applied an appropriate color of lipstick. My shoes were free of debris and polished. Feeling like I had a fighting chance of looking respectable, I entered the church early and found Tellie with only one other person paying her respects. When their conversation had ended, I approached Tellie, softly calling her name.

Tellie turned. She studied me with unbridled mistrust. "Josiah, how nice of you to come," she said stiffly.

"Should I be sorry for your loss?" Damn it. Couldn't I have said something less antagonistic?

She snorted. "You still have that sharp tongue. One of these days, it's going to cut you."

I tried a more subtle approach. "Tellie, I *am* truly sorry for your loss. I know what it is to lose someone."

"Yes, Brannon. Wasn't he living with a much younger woman when he died?"

I flinched. "Let's bury the hatchet, okay? I don't want to make trouble but I do think we need to talk."

"About what?"

"Some strange things have been happening to me. I thought maybe you might know something about them."

"Why should that concern me? I really don't care what has been happening to you."

"Even if it involves Taffy?"

Tellie started to speak but stopped, as Taffy and Nancy strolled into the church, both attired like Goth vampire girls.

Barely stifling a low groan, Tellie's face revealed hostility mixed with pain. So she didn't like Nancy. This was part of the stuff I had come here to learn.

The two approached us. Taffy was certainly in a grief mode, as if it suddenly had dawned on her that her father was really dead. Her eyes were red from crying. Nancy just looked ridiculous tagging along.

"What are you doing here?" Nancy asked me.

"Paying my respects."

"I'd be ashamed to come here after Taffy's daddy died on your property and all," retorted Nancy. Taffy glanced nervously at Nancy.

"Well, I guess that is the difference between grown-up behavior and just weird behavior. You goin' to a Halloween party after this?"

"Both of you, shut up," hissed Tellie. "This service is for my daughter and myself. If you can't behave yourselves, then get the hell out of here."

I mumbled my apologies. Silently asking God to forgive me, I went to sit in the back of the church. I was well aware that Tellie seemed to have a newfound confidence, which had never been displayed when Richard was alive. This interested me. What caused the mouse to turn into . . . at least, a lion cub?

From the back pew, I had an ideal vantage point from which to study those who came to pay their respects. Gray-haired men, who looked like retirees from IBM, offered their condolences to Tellie. Afterwards, they stood chatting in little pods. I listened to several of the men compare war stories about their IBM careers. Ever so often, Richard's name would be mentioned. A short silence always followed.

Members of the Farmers' Market began to make their appearances. Even Otto Brown, who had bothered to shave and put on his Sunday suit with a clean starched shirt, showed up, with Mrs. Brown, in a brightly colored caftan, following faithfully behind. I watched Otto pat Tellie's hand a little too long while talking to her and wondered what Mrs. Brown thought of this. Tellie put her hand in her dress pocket.

"No fool like an old fool, I always say." I looked up to see Irene Meckler, my buddy from the Farmers' Market, standing in the aisle. "Did you see old man Brown try to paw Tellie with his wife standing right there." Irene shook her head. "Disgusting."

I scooted over for Irene to join me. "Hey Irene. Just get here?"

Irene pushed her glasses up on her sharply pointed nose. "You don't think I'd miss this, do you," she guffawed. "I must say that Tellie is looking awfully smart."

"Yes, it is ironic to see how pretty she looks today of all days."

"What's that getup Taffy got on? She looks like early Madonna."

Not knowing what to say, I just shook my head.

Irene sniggered. "Oh my God, there's another one dressed like an eighties reject."

I looked piously at a prayer book, as I knew people were looking to see who was snickering.

"Shh," I cautioned Irene out of the corner of my mouth. "Don't get us thrown out of church."

Irene began coughing and opened her large purse to find a mint. "Chest cold," rasped Irene to an irritated woman turning around to see who was causing the commotion. My friend whispered conspiratorially, "Guess who was pulling into the parking lot as I was coming up the steps?"

"Haven't a clue."

"Agnes Bledsoe."

"This ought to be interesting."

Irene and I both settled in to watch the show. Other farmers, seeing us, sat nearby, providing a cocoon of solidarity. Apparently, they decided to give me a show of support. I was glad. They also provided a screen from which I could observe unobtrusively. While nodding and giving appropriate responses to comments flying my way, I watched Agnes Bledsoe make her way up to the altar and intently scrutinize pictures of Richard on display. Occasionally pausing before a particular picture, she studied it, sometimes touching it gently with her fingertips.

Agnes had told me that she and Tellie had never met, so I watched with great interest as Agnes greeted Tellie. They spoke for a moment and then Agnes moved back to the pictures. Tellie gave no sign of recognition as she moved to receive other guests. I wondered what name Agnes had given her. To my great astonishment, Agnes pilfered one of the pictures, cupped it in her hand against her suit skirt and walked out of the church.

Taffy and Tellie, unaware of the picture theft, continued talking. There went one of my theories that Tellie and Agnes were in on it together.

"Well," I said to Irene. "Agnes told at least one truth. She and Tellie had never met. Tellie didn't know who Agnes was."

"Agnes sure left in a hurry. I guess so nobody from the old days might pepper her with questions," replied Irene. "She shouldn't have taken that picture. She should have asked Tellie for it."

I should have known that nothing missed Irene's hawk-like eyes. "Agnes told me that she was leaving her estate to Taffy." I left out the bit about Agnes' cancer.

Irene was thoughtful for a moment. "I guess there's justice in that. God knows, she and Tellie will need it eventually. I think Richard was about to go belly-up . . . financially, I mean."

"There's no money in bees," I confirmed. "It's labor intensive and the profit margin is too low to make any money."

"It would just seem that Richard would have kept the first dollar he ever made."

"Maybe he spent it all on cleaning products," I said sarcastically.

Out of the corner of my eye, I saw Larry Bingham make his way up the aisle to Tellie. I watched keenly as they talked. Tellie shook her head after Larry thrust an envelope into her hand. Without waiting, he turned, leaving the church by the side door. Larry had looked relieved, as though he had just executed a solemn duty and was now free from its burden. He didn't notice me huddled in my little nest of farmers and I made no effort to let him know that I was present. Didn't he tell me that he had left the beekeepers' check in Tellie's mailbox? What was in the envelope?

Feeling a little like Hercule Poirot, I was mentally checking off suspects in my private drama. So far everyone had acted true to his or her nature. Agnes, aloof and proud, stole a picture of Richard, leaving without saying a word to anyone. Otto, who disliked Richard, took his anger out on the widow by subtly pawing her at the dead man's memorial service. Taffy, the not-too-bright daughter, was dressed in mourning black to be sure, but in a circus freak sort of way. Her companion Nancy, in a bid to control an already dysfunctional relationship, was barking orders. Only Tellie, the long-suffering wife, usually meek and quiet, seemed confident and composed. Yes, it was only Tellie who seemed out of character.

The organ started playing, jolting me out of my fugue. We all stood, grabbing hymnals and searching for the designated hymn. No one ever liked singing hymns at funerals. They were usually dreary. I crossed my fingers, hoping that we would not have to sing *Amazing Grace*. I wearied of it as much as I did of *The Old Rugged Cross*. Instead, we sang about the tides of sin being washed up from the raging sea upon the calm shore of forgiveness. What the sea had to do with Richard, I could not guess.

True to most Baptist funerals, the preacher talked about Richard finding salvation after being baptized in water – a very big deal for us Baptists. Now that he had been reborn in the blood of the Lamb, Richard rested in the bosom of Jesus, no matter how much of a jerk he was in life. The minister didn't utter those exact words, but his meaning was clear. Then the Twenty-third Psalm was read as it has been read at every funeral I have ever attended.

Years ago, I made my daughter promise that Psalm Twenty-three would never be read at my funeral. It's not that God doesn't watch over us. It just seems he is very picky as to whom he will help. Benjamin Franklin was right when he espoused that God helps those who help themselves – in other words, don't sit waiting for heavenly help. It might not come.

Straining my neck, I tried to see Tellie. She sat serenely in the front pew along with Taffy, who sobbed quietly into her handkerchief. Still as a sphinx, Tellie sat beside her grieving daughter, staring at the preacher. I wondered if she was holding Taffy's hand. Thank goodness Nancy had chosen to sit in a back pew.

I wondered how I would have acted at Brannon's funeral. My daughter and I will never know since we didn't have one. Devastated by the lack of regard for us in his will, I just collected his ashes, storing them in my closet. I didn't even purchase an urn. He's in a cardboard box. His girlfriend had a service for him.

My daughter and I had left town that week to avoid the gossip and hard questions that would have surely come our way. Maybe that was why I had been so depressed for the past three years. I never had closure with Brannon. Never gone through the rituals that officially would put the past behind me. Brannon Sr. was sitting in my closet – waiting, waiting.

Besotted by love, Brannon had turned his back on his wife and first-born. Besotted by love, I abandoned Brannon in

158

death. I felt it had been an even trade.

I wondered how Tellie felt. Did she regret her marriage to Richard or was she just sad about how things had turned out – mean and trivial?

The invitation was given for those who wished to give testimony about Richard's life. Embarrassingly, no one came forward until two members from the Beekeepers Association stepped up and gave a glowing report of how Richard was a rare bee charmer who tended his hives well, which was ironic to everyone since Richard had died while being stung by countless bees. After they sat down, an uncomfortable silence filled the sanctuary.

Irene chuckled softly. While Irene was most sympathetic to Tellie and Taffy, she had no use for the man who used to tell Market customers that her flowers were nothing more than weeds. She poked me with her elbow and gave me a knowing look that said, "You reap what you sow."

Bored, I glanced about the church only to discover Detective O'nan sitting several pews behind Tellie on the opposite side. Instinctively, I sank in the pew. Realizing that I was acting like a fool, I raised my head. O'nan was turned in his seat glaring at me. I swallowed hard while averting my eyes. I tried to not let O'nan intimidate me . . . but he did. I was afraid of him. I wished I was a brave swashbuckler like Errol Flynn freeing his chained mates in *The Sea Hawk*. But the truth was that I was a middle-aged, overweight woman with asthma, no fighting skills and no protector. I had only my wits to shelter me from an increasingly hostile world. I wrestled with the notion of calling Matt but decided against it. I had bothered Matt enough. I didn't want to become a burden.

Sensing my apprehension, Irene asked, "Who's that guy looking at you?"

"He was the cop in charge of Richard's case."

"Was?"

"Well, the death has been listed as a heart attack."

Miriam, the peach lady, eavesdropping, leaned forward from the pew behind us and asked, "What was Richard doing at your place? Everybody's wondering."

"I honestly don't know," I replied, happy that I could truthfully answer. Before I could be asked another question, I excused myself to use the restroom. I really did have to use the bathroom. Finding them near the Sunday school rooms in the basement, I did my business, washed my hands and freshened up my lipstick, although the fresh coat managed to look drab under the fluorescent lights.

I didn't anticipate finding O'nan leaning against the opposite wall with his arms folded when I came out. I hissed like a scalded cat. "You are under orders not to have contact with me," I said quickly.

"Don't know what you are talking about. Just wanted to use the washroom. How was I to know that you were coming out of the only one?"

"Because you followed me." As I started past O'nan, he blocked my way and pressed against me. I felt his chest heavy against my breasts. Trying to free myself from his touch, I managed only to back up further in the dark hallway. "Stand away," I managed to say firmly. "I'm warning you." My heart was thumping hard against my rib cage.

O'nan kept inching towards me. I backed up only to find myself trapped in a dead-end hallway. I fumbled for a light switch with no luck. Now both of us were in the shadows.

O'nan pushed me against the wall, his hands fumbling at my dress buttons. Slapping his hands away caused O'nan to smile at my heightening distress. "I was surprised when you didn't remember me, Professor Reynolds, but then why would you? My friends and I were nothing to you. You didn't care that you might ruin our lives. I lost my scholarship and my chance at pro ball because of you."

"You made the decision to cheat. You got what you deserved."

He pressed his cheek against mine whispering into my ear. "You have never cheated? Aw come on – never? Never on your taxes . . . never fudged on an application form? Never took a pen that didn't belong to you? Never cheated on your husband?" O'nan ran his tongue down my cheek.

"Oh," I cried. "Stop."

He nibbled my ear. I could feel his arousal through his clothes.

"I'll scream."

O'nan laughed. "I'm betting on it."

My eyes flew open. He was making no attempt to contain my hands. This was a trap, an attempt for me to hit him so he could charge me with assault.

There would be no marks on me, but he would have some. It would be my word against his version of what had occurred – great copy for the newspapers.

"I know your game," I said turning my lips towards his. "You're trying to get me to slap you. What were you going to say – that I slugged you coming out of the bathroom? That I took a poke at you? Nobody would believe the story that I was protecting myself from being molested. I mean – it sounds ludicrous. I look like a run-down clock. Why would a young buck try to accost an old bag like me? Well, baby, I've got news for you. It has been a long time since a man touched me – so you go right ahead. Do your worst. I won't hit you. I won't even scream." I reached down and fumbled with his belt.

O'nan pushed himself away from me. "You're crazy!"

"What I am is smart. I was smarter than you when I was your professor and I'm smarter than you now. Only a doofus would come up with such a ridiculous plan. I didn't ruin your life, buddy boy; you did that all by yourself. Quit blaming me. How you ever made detective is beyond me. So if you are not going to screw me, then get out of my way."

"You're scared of me. You're trembling."

"More like shuddering. Your stupidity frightens me."

"I know you killed Richard Pidgeon, and I'm going to prove it."

"Haven't you heard that the case is closed? Even if the case were still open, you have been dismissed. You'll never get close to Richard's case again."

"We'll see about that."

"This from a man who can't even tell an El Greco from a Dali," I sneered, surging past O'nan. *Please don't have an asthma attack now,* I said to myself as I walked towards the staircase. I could feel O'nan's eyes scrutinizing me, wishing me to stumble, perhaps falling down and breaking my neck. I would never give that idiot the satisfaction.

Re-entering the sanctuary, I saw Irene walking towards me. "I was getting concerned," she said, peering over her glasses. "Thought maybe something was wrong." She studied me. "You look awfully pale, Josiah."

I didn't reply.

"Everyone is going home. How about we go for a drink?"

"Yeah, that sounds good. I'll follow you in my van," I replied. My skin felt clammy and my knees were weak. What I needed was Dutch courage before I faced my isolated house on the palisades. I hated funerals and made up my mind not to attend any more – including my own.

21

Working bees is sheer toil. They do not take kindly to someone opening their hives to steal the product of their hard work of collecting nectar. It takes the nectar from two million flowers just to make one pound of honey – so you can see their point of view concerning the honey harvesting issue. But if they are handled gently with lots of smoke, the collateral damage can be small – on both sides. I was on an exploratory expedition searching for disease or anything in the hives that was funky, trying to get them ready for winter.

I pressed my knee against the back of the hive. If the hive remained stable, then it had enough honey for the winter. If the hive tilted forward, the bees would have to be fed.

It was almost dusk when I came to the hive that Richard's head had been stuffed into like a fat sardine. I checked it carefully as the bees were still skittish. They had never sufficiently recovered from the stress and damage of that day. I went to get a portable nuc, placing the frames with bees from the main hive into the smaller box. A nuc is a miniature hive. I poured a line of honey on each frame to distract the bees.   After cramming the nuc with the Queen and thirty thousand worker bees, I put the top on.

I checked the empty hive body for stragglers.   Satisfied, I placed the nuc and the old hive into the van and proceeded to the trash-burning area.   I positioned the van close to the burn pile.   After placing the empty hive boxes on the pile, I got the nuc out, placing it on the van hood so the bees could see out. I lit the old hive boxes on fire, while the bees and I watched the bad juju burn away.   I patted the nuc.   "Don't worry. I've got a great new place for you tomorrow morning. "

The humming of the bees swelled and then lulled into a nice cooing.

After banking the dying fire, I placed the nuc of bees back in the van.   Tomorrow, I would take them to their new home in Madison County, where I had another beeyard on a friend's farm.   Since the blue moon was bright, I went back to where the compromised hive had been.   Carefully, I poured salt on the ground, chanting a medieval prayer for bees.   Then, using a large branch, I raked the salt into the soil.   My smoker was still lit so I smudged the entire area.   Satisfied that the yard had been cleansed of all bad energy, I lay in the tall grass listening to the night sounds and fell asleep studying the celestial canopy.

Awaking several hours later, wet with dew and stiff with the night cold eating at my arthritic bones, I pulled my rigid limbs up from the ground and limped towards home following the pools of moonlight scattered on the gravel road. Not wanting to get the bees rattled again, I hadn't started the van.   I didn't mind the half-mile trek to the house, but wished I had my walking stick.   About two hundred feet ahead, a coyote ran out on to the road, stopping to inspect me.   Friend or foe?   Either I was too big to take down or getting a whiff of my human smell, she decided in favor of caution and disappeared into the bushes. But it wasn't me that the coyote was cautious of – it was something else.

I was quiet like the coyote, which is why Nancy and Taffy didn't hear me behind them. My heart gave a start when I saw two human forms sneaking down the road. I hunkered on the wet ground until they turned a corner, and then followed behind trying to hear their conversation. Excitedly, they whispered to each other as they tiptoed around trees that lined the gravel driveway. It had probably been the sound of their car that had awakened me. In Nancy's hand, I spied what appeared to be a gas can. *Those lunatics!*

I was sick of their psycho behavior and mystified as to what good they thought their hostile actions would do them. I knew that I couldn't handle them by myself. I didn't know if Matt was in the cabana or not. I had fallen asleep before he got home. He could just as well be having a night out with Franklin.

I was on my own. Pulling out my cell phone, I began to call the police but decided against it. Fury welled up within me. I was mad as hell and wasn't going to take it anymore. Calculating the risks of revenge coming back to bite me in the butt, I surmised that it could be low. It was time to inflict some grief of my own.

Brannon was right. I could be quite nasty when I wanted to be. Their car had to be parked at the front gate. I faded into the shadows, backtracking to the entrance of my property. Puffing, I made it to the gate. Thank goodness I had my albuterol spray with me.

Sitting pretty for me was Nancy's car. I didn't even think about what I was doing. It was like I was on automatic pilot. I slowly climbed the gate as the keypad was on the other side.

Pulling out my cell phone, I called the police telling them there were intruders trying to get into my home and it looked like they had weapons. They had to come quick. The dispatcher was still talking to me when I shut the phone. Unzipping my beesuit, I tore off a piece of my T- shirt, stuffing it in the gas tank. Teeth chattering, I lit the shirt with my Zippo lighter. I felt the adrenaline coursing through me as I entered the gate code. As soon as the gate opened a little, I was through it as if the devil himself was after me. I ran to the field where my van was stationed, nicely hidden by a stand of apple trees.

It wasn't long until there was a big boom with the sky lighting up like a Fourth of July jamboree. I waited as the shadowy figures of Taffy and Nancy ran past me. What a surprise waited for them. Knowing they were distraught and screaming, I started my van, keeping the lights off, and drove through the fields until I could get back on the driveway.

Making another call to the police, I reported an explosion and said that it looked like a fire had been set on my property. I also gave a description of two females. The dispatcher told me to stay on the phone until the police arrived and to stay in the house.

"Oh, no, here they come again! I can see them through the window," I cried before turning off the phone again. Racing the car to the house, I threw open the front door and turned on the lights. Running into my bedroom, I tore off my dew-sweat-stained beesuit and boots. Frantically, I grabbed a sweatshirt from the back of my closet. After getting out my taser baton, I checked on Baby in his crate. He was agitated but all right.

Merde – the gate! The police can't get in. I called again. The dispatcher, now angry that she kept getting cut off, ordered me to stay on the line. She reported that the police had found a burning car by the front gate but they couldn't get onto the property. I gave her the code and several minutes later, I saw the flashing lights of the men in blue. I was actually happy to see them this time. Officers stepped out of their cruisers and lowered their heads as if any moment a spray of bullets would come their way.

"Stay in the house," they yelled. I slammed the door shut.

Twenty minutes later, I opened the door in response to a firm knock. Standing in my doorway were four handsome policemen holding two handcuffed, disarrayed women –Taffy and Nancy. "We caught them." One of the officers held up a red gasoline can. "They had this," he added. "Looks like they were going to burn you out. You know them?"

"Yes, I'm sorry to say that I do."

"You set my car on fire!" screamed Nancy.

"You're the one holding a gasoline can," mused the officer in charge.

"What was on fire?" I asked.

"A car which they say is theirs."

"No other brush fires on the property?"

"The fire department is going through the property right now. Perhaps you would like to show them your property line."

I certainly would. I got in a police car and was soon joined by more husky young men doing their best to protect me from two "lawbreakers" who were now stuffed into the back of a police van.

Nancy stared out of the back window at us passing by.

"I wonder if that girl is really crazy?" I said. "Why would she set her own car on fire?"

"My guess is so that you would come out of the house to investigate."

"Then what?"

"They also had duct tape."

"Oooh," I said faintly. "They weren't kidding around." I didn't point out to the officer that the girls had no way to get home. Maybe he had seen so much criminal stupidity that he didn't question this angle. Perhaps he thought they would just steal my van after they were finished with me.

Finished with me! That had a horrible ring to it. What was the purpose of the duct tape? Tie me to a chair while they poured gasoline over me? Would Taffy really go that far? The police evidently thought so.

I gave an officer my statement about how I was in my house when I heard unusual sounds and the motion lights came on. I was completely believable when I described how I looked out the window, seeing two shadowy figures lurking outside, one of them holding something large in her hands. I called the police the first time. Then I heard the explosion. The police seemed satisfied with my story. I also mentioned that Taffy's father had died on my property some months ago. Perhaps this was an attempt at revenge? Just a suggestion. I was enjoying myself. I should have taken up lying earlier in life as a hobby.

After the police left, I let Baby out of his crate and fed him some sliced roast beef. Heating up a Lean Cuisine dinner for myself, I topped if off with a quart of chocolate ice cream. The Baptist in me knew I was going to hell, but the problem was I didn't feel guilty about how I had set those girls up. It seemed like they were going to do worse to me. I shuddered when I thought of the duct tape and its possible use with the gasoline. Was Taffy so *daffy* that she thought I really killed her father and wanted revenge? Where was Daffy Taffy's mother in all this mess?

So much for getting rid of bad karma.

22

My mother taught me to never judge a book by its cover but I do . . . doesn't everyone? I should have known better that things on the outside may look differently at its core. It's not like I didn't have real life lessons in this.

At the age of six, Brannon attended a party at the home of his neighborhood's avant-garde couple. The husband was a hip radio announcer of a jazz show while his beautiful wife was a noted songwriter of the Carole King ilk. They threw parties to which they invited fascinating people to their street's upper-middle-class world of Swanson TV dinners and Ed Sullivan on Sunday nights. As they had a child Brannon's age, Brannon was allowed to participate by being a companion to his friend if they could prove themselves to be charming entertainment for what was really the cast of an Andy Warhol party . . . be cute but not obnoxiously apparent.

Apparently, one of the guests did not think the cherubic attitude was something that he wished to condone. A waxed mustachioed man called Brannon over, telling him to hold out his hand. Thinking he was going to receive money or maybe candy, little Brannon was more than happy to extend his plump greedy little palm towards the gentleman who was smoking a Turkish cigarette in a long cigarette holder. The gentleman grandly took his cigarette holder out of his mouth and flicked ashes in Brannon's hand. "Now go away, little boy," he requested.

Astonished, Brannon took the ashes to show his friend. Even at that age, Brannon realized the man was trying to insult him. Wiping his hands on his friend's clean shirt, Brannon stomped home crying.

It wasn't until years later that he realized that he had been given a treasure – a vintage slice of life with Lord Buckley, the famous Beat comedian, which could be retold at countless dinner parties, cocktail parties and business dinners, never failing to make him look charming or bring a smile even to the dullest face at the table. I mean, who doesn't like to hear about children being humiliated by a hip fifties comedian whose battle cry was "hipsters, flipsters and finger poppin' daddies, knock me your lobes"?

I have taken this story to heart . . . that something nasty can turn out to be a trove of enchantment. *I am still looking for the silver lining in Brannon's treachery, but it may still come.* It was with this attitude that I went to the Fayette County hoosegow, which looks like a horse barn, to see Taffy after she had called me. She had something important to tell me.

"Tell me on the phone," I had said.

"No, I got to see you, Miss Josiah," she replied. "Got to tell you in person."

Figuring that she was going to try to get me to drop the charges, I pulled my resolve together and proceeded to the jailhouse in my rickety van. I hoped that it was not merely a setup, only to come out to find my van stolen from the jail's parking lot; I knew Nancy was already out on bail. I wondered why Taffy was not. It was going to be an interesting chat, as I waited patiently while my body and purse were wanded before I entered the core of the building. I got the feeling lots of people bring tape recorders as the guard pulled mine out, looked at it, looked at me and put it back. He whispered something as he handed the purse back to me. I nodded, but had no real clue as to what he was saying. I guess the guards worried more about guns, blades and drugs smuggled in.

Not that the Bluegrass area is a hotbed of crime, but we do have our share of citizens who name their little girls Adolf Hitler, take in fifty cats and then forget to feed them, participate in illegal cockfights, tuck marijuana plants away in our state parks and leave mutilated bodies by the river. Most of our murders are alcohol-driven domestic affairs, usually relatives killing their dearly loved ones. Kentuckians get angry when the outside world stereotypes us as violent or stupid, but sometimes the stereotype fits. Now I was going to meet one of its queens – Daffy Taffy.

I checked into the lounge bathroom in order to switch on the recorder, then proceeded down the hall where I would meet Taffy. Unfortunately, it was a large room where the prisoners could mingle with the visitors. I was hoping for a thick glass wall with hand phones. Taffy was sitting in an orange plastic chair tugging at her hair, looking absent-mindedly at the cement floor.

I walked up to her. "Hello, Taffy. You wanted to see me."

She gave me a quick nod and showed me to a scarred table that stood away from everyone.

"It's nice that you came . . . considering," said Taffy.

"I admit I thought it odd that you called me. Why are you

172

still here? Why aren't you out on bail?"

Taffy had the grace to look ashamed. "Mommy won't get me out. Says for me to stay here until she is ready. Ready for what is what I would like to know." She looked around at the other inmates visiting their families. "I want out. I hate this place."

"I hope you're not asking me to get you out."

Taffy looked sheepishly at me. "I know you think I'm a bad girl."

"I think you were going to harm me is what I think."

"Oh no, that wasn't the plan," Taffy said quickly.

I put the tape recorder on the table. "Well, before we come to what you want, we are going to do a little horse trading. Tell me what I want to know and then we'll see if I help you at all."

"That seems fair. I tell you what you want, then you'll call my mother and talk to her?"

"I won't make that promise. I have to see, but if you don't answer my questions with the truth, then I won't do anything at all except try to see that the police keep you here. Where is that nutter friend of yours – Nancy?"

"She had some money saved up and paid her bail. She didn't have enough for me too." Taffy rubbed her forehead. "She's the cause of all this mess. I wish I had never met her."

"I just want you to know that I have alerted the Fayette County District Attorney that I am meeting you. If anything happens to my farm while I'm here . . then they will pick up little Miss Nancy again." It was true that I had told Officer Kelly about this meeting and he agreed to watch my property while I was on my little mission.

"This is on the up and up, Miss Josiah. I swear. I'll do what you want. Ask me anything. Just help me with my mother."

I turned on the tape recorder. "Why have you been harassing me – the letters, the car accident?"

Taffy paled.

So I was right – she was not denying the letters or the accident.

"I don't know why really. Daddy's death on your farm. I didn't understand why he would be there. And there was the incident where you pushed him into a glass case. I can't explain it. I was just angry. I didn't really mean any harm. It was Nancy that goaded me into writing the letters," she gushed.

"And Brutus is an honorable man," I quoted sarcastically.

"Huh?"

"First of all, I did push your father but only after he had pushed me. I don't take kindly to men bullying women. It makes me mad. But I had nothing to do with your father's death. I had no idea that he was on my property and that he was in need of any type of medical assistance. Had I known, I would have tried to help him. To that, I will swear on the Bible. I had nothing to do with your daddy's death."

"Nancy said you had to have something to do with it, and that you were getting away with it because you're rich and your daughter has connections."

"Let's leave my daughter out of this. Nancy is wrong. It wasn't me."

"Oh."

"Why did you use a typewriter?"

"The printer for my laptop was broken so I used Daddy's old typewriter."

"What is your relationship with Nurse Nancy?"

Taffy shrugged. "She's into chicks."

"Are you?"

"Not really, but I was between boyfriends . . . and I thought – what the hell. I was willing to experiment."

"How has it been?"

"At first, it was good." She grinned. "And the sex wasn't too difficult to get used to. In fact, it was fun but she is so bossy. Nancy has all these weird ideas about people. She had been pushed around a lot between foster homes and such when she was little, so she hates anyone who has it better. I'm not like that."

"So from what you are telling me, all these ideas were from Nancy, and you went along with them?" I asked to clarify. I was going to point out that Nancy was old enough to be her mother but I am sure that Tellie had already had this conversation with Taffy.

"I couldn't say no to her. There was no point. She'd just keep badgering me until I gave in," Taffy pouted.

"Did it ever occur to you to talk to me?"

"No, I'm sorry. Now I know I should have."

"Those letters you sent about my husband were hurtful. They also kept the cops on my ass."

"That's how Nancy knew you. She said she was a nurse when your husband was sick and you were so mean to him that you caused him to die. She was so sure you had something to do with Daddy's death too."

"My husband died from a coronary episode which stemmed from heart disease. Did she tell you that he had a mistress who led him to desert his daughter and me?"

"She didn't put it that way."

"Of course not, it depends on whose viewpoint you take. He never thought of the pain he was causing his wife and daughter. He just cared about his new squeeze. Let's not waste time on my late husband. So far, I've got that you were having an affair with Nancy Wasser because you were bored and she talked you into believing that I had something to do with your father's death. Does that get it?"

Taffy nodded, her cheeks a hot pink.

"Say yes or no."

"I would say that sounds about right."

"That the two of you conspired to write letters to the police and to myself accusing me of killing your father and my husband?"

"I didn't think it would really do you harm," whined Taffy. "I just wanted the police to investigate, just to be sure, you know."

"Why the old English in the last letter?"

"Nancy thought it would throw suspicion off from us. That's all."

"And that the two of you thought it was okay to push me to the brink of death by driving my Mercedes off the road after the Harvest Ball."

"I had nothing to do with that."

"Did Nancy?"

"No."

"The two of you had nothing to do with chasing me down on Ironworks Pike and forcing my car into a fence?"

"No!"

"How do you know Nancy didn't? How do you explain the fact that her car has a dent in the front?" I lied.

"We were at the ball together. You saw us. She never went after you."

"Were you two together the entire night after Matt and I left?"

Taffy looked at the guard and mouthed that she wanted to leave. I grabbed her hand.

176

"Answer me, Taffy, or I will not help you with your mother."

The guard shifted his feet while placing his hand on his pepper spray. He shook his head at me. I pulled my hand away.

"Well, we were going to leave too. She said she had to go to the bathroom and then she was going to get the car."

"Whose car?"

"My Mom's. She was using our new car that night and I was to use her old one."

"She was using the Prius?"

"Yes."

"Okay, so you were using your mom's old car, the Suburban. Was Nancy gone a long time?"

"She said she had trouble finding the bathroom. The line was long so she decided to warm the car up for me and drive it closer to the front door and then went to use the bathroom."

"That didn't seem odd to you?"

"No, she could be thoughtful like that."

"Did your mother's car have any scratches or dents?"

"Never looked."

"Your mother say anything?"

"No, except that she didn't want me to see Nancy no more. She warned me that Nancy was no good and would get me into trouble." Taffy started to sniffle. "She was right. Look where I am."

"Okay. Let's go back. Nancy went to the bathroom, got lost and then went to get the car, letting it warm up. So she was gone fifteen to twenty-five minutes," I said, putting the pieces together.

"Yeah."

"Or even thirty minutes?"

"I dunno. I wasn't watching the clock."

"Could she have been gone thirty minutes?"

"Maybe."

"What about coming to my house with a gas can and duct tape?"

"That was just a prank really to get you back for the way you and Matt treated us at the ball. Nancy said you insulted us and then you took off with our drink glasses. Nancy didn't like that. At the most, I thought we'd set some shed on fire."

"Whose idea was it to bring the duct tape?"

"Nancy's," answered Taffy distractedly while picking dirt from underneath her fingernails.

Snapping my fingers, I said, "Taffy, stay with me. What was the tape for?"

"Never asked."

I leaned back in my chair. "You poor dumb kid. Don't you realize that bringing duct tape made it look like you were going to murder me?"

"No, no. We were just gonna scare you."

I shook my head in disgust. "You didn't think to hide your identity which indicates you were planning not to leave any witnesses. Taffy, you're in serious trouble, don't you realize this? I haven't talked with the DA yet, but there is a strong chance that you might be charged with attempted murder. Aren't you worried that Nancy might roll over on you in order to make a deal?"

"Huh?" Taffy's eyes grew large with tears. "I just wanted to scare you. That's what Nancy said we was gonna do. Just a prank. I swear to you, Miss Josiah. Oh, I wish I had listened to Mommy."

"For goodness sakes, Taffy, that Nancy woman is a psycho. You do well to do what your mother tells you. Did you have anything to do with your father's death?"

Taffy blanched and swallowed hard. "No, how can you ask such a thing? I know my father had some serious problems, but I loved him." She looked at me sheepishly. "Hated him too, but I could never hurt him. I just wanted to get as far away from him as possible."

"How do you think your father died?"

"Heart attack. I just thought maybe you upset him when he came out to your place and caused his heart to fail like Nancy said you did to your husband."

"Is that what your mother thinks?"

"That's what Mommy told me."

"Do you know where your mother was the morning of your father's death?"

"She was at work like always and then home at her regular time. Why do you ask?"

"Nothing. I will speak to your mother, but I don't know that I will ask the charges to be dropped. Some restitution will have to be made. You have cost me a lot of money, not to mention sleepless nights."

"I'm sorry," said Taffy, wiping her nose with her sleeve.

"Sorry doesn't cut it." I stood up. "We'll see what happens, Taffy, but your mother is right. You need to be on a short leash." I left without saying goodbye or looking back. I just wanted to go home. I knew Taffy believed me. The problem was that if another person came along after I left and told her that I had killed her father, she would believe that person too. Taffy believed anyone who had just last talked to her. No wonder Nancy could persuade her to do anything. Stupidly, I felt sorry for Daffy Taffy.

23

It is a hard thing to witness frantic drones struggling to get back in the hive as they are being stung to death by worker bees that once fed and groomed them. But if the hive wants to survive, the females of the hive need to live through the winter, so the male drones are expendable and gotten rid of in the most brutal of ways, killed by their loved ones. Love stinks.

For a crime that had not been committed as declared by the Kentucky medical examiner, I surely had suffered as though I had been guilty. I had had my house ransacked by the police, a thirty-thousand-dollar piece of art glass broken, spent forty thousand on security doodads, paid penalties and taxes to break my IRA, been run off the road by a crazy nurse, had threatening letters sent to me, been groped by a cop who hated me, spent several thousand dollars for fingerprint/DNA tests on letters accusing me of murder, had one car towed, another one totaled, gave my criminal lawyer an expensive painting to cover my fees, spent a three-thousand-dollar night in the hospital, and was now selling ten acres of my land to get me out of the financial mess that had been dumped on me through no fault of my own. This did not include my purchase of a puppy that would grow to two hundred pounds and was showing signs of being extremely willful. In addition, my helper had taken up permanent residence, rent-free, in my caretaker's bungalow.

As I worked my honeybees, I wondered what Richard's death would have cost me had I really been guilty of murdering him. It probably would have been cheaper just to confess and go to trial. I finished feeding two weak hives with bee pollen goo. It was a warm October day with the trees just at their riotous height of color. Finished with my tasks, I walked back to the Butterfly and, once inside, pulled off my thick gloves and grabbed the iced tea from the fridge. Ahh – sweet iced tea, the wine of the south.

Some people would argue that Kentucky is not the South, that it is a border state with its own unique culture. I guess they don't understand the Mason-Dixon line. They had never come to Lexington at Derby time and stayed in fine old mansions that African slaves and poor Irish had built – many of which my husband had restored to their former glory and then some.

Lexington has always been very southern in its manners but split in its politics. When I first moved to Lexington from northern Kentucky, Lexingtonians still revered the Confederate John Hunt Morgan and had preserved the house in which he rode his horse into the parlor to kiss his mother goodbye before going out on a raid. Every day, people passed by the site where Cassius Clay wrote his abolitionist paper several streets over from where his distant cousin Henry Clay, the Great Compromiser, shot craps on the side of his law office while slaves ran his estate. Though the Visitor's Center downplays Cheapside Park, everyone knows it was the location of one of the busiest slave markets in the South. Many old families still have ambrotypes of Cheapside in its heyday with white men bidding on a multitude of darker-skinned people. And sometimes, free people of color also bid on those who came to the auction block or an occasional white person who had sold themselves into servitude.

Take the story of a white man, William "King" Solomon, who was purchased by a freed slave by the name of Aunt Charlotte for the price of eighteen cents. She was a respectable baker who specialized in cakes and pies. Solomon was the town drunk. Somehow, they struck a chord with one another. Solomon dutifully carried out his duties of fetching wood and maintaining her stoves so Miss Charlotte could bake, and she provided a decent place for Solomon to sleep. She even cared enough about him that when a cholera epidemic broke out in 1833, she begged him to escape with her before the illness struck them both down. He refused, sending Miss Charlotte to safety, while he stayed to bury the bodies of the deceased. Steadfast through the cholera epidemic, he buried the dead for the town of Lexington. The town drunk is today considered a hero of Lexington.

Like "King" Solomon, Lexington has two personalities – that of the conservative suburban element that votes staunchly Democrat for governor and Republican for president, and the downtown liberal bohemian art scene of writers, artists and actors. They never seem to bump into each other except on Gallery Hop night. It is perhaps good manners that each group just looks the other way. Our unofficial motto was live-and-let-live, that is until Lexington began to grow from sixty thousand to three hundred thousand people.

It was during the late seventies and early eighties, the influx of Yankees and Eastern Kentucky immigrants caused the Bluegrass to overrun itself with a glut of ticky-tacky housing developments. Like the newcomers, I also was an immigrant to the Bluegrass and as guilty as the carpetbaggers devouring the South after the Civil War. Cashing in on the real estate boom ourselves, Brannon and I were flush with money from his restoring antebellum houses and designing new ones for the out-of-town nouveau riche investing in race horses. Brannon was becoming nationally known, and I was on my way to tenure at UK. We thought the building boom would go on forever and bust was a four-letter word. I didn't care that I was harming a sensitive environment. I was too ambitious.

In our early days together, we had an apartment in town. These were the times when the rich and famous flitted in and out of Lexington like gilded butterflies. Henry Faulkner was still alive, driving around with his goat and happened to live on our street. He liked us, so we would be invited to his informal parties where Tennessee Williams sat drunk, mumbling in a corner or Bette Davis argued with Henry about his chili recipe. One could walk down the street and pass Rock Hudson or Sweet Evening Breeze on the same evening – or so it was rumored around town.

There seemed to be a riotous party all the time. People knew how to have fun. Even during the weekday, people socialized at cocktail or dinner parties. Rich horse people gave famous Derby parties. Britain's Princess Margaret stayed with the Whitneys. IBM was the major employer in the city besides the University of Kentucky. And everyone knew everyone else.

Not anymore. IBM left town. Some of the rich gave up

their parties and became real estate moguls. Princess Margaret died. I hardly know anybody when I go to a function now. Everyone is younger than I. But I had saved 139 acres of prime Bluegrass that included a pristine palisades eco-system. That was my atonement.

Sipping on my sweet tea, I put on a *Big Maybelle* CD and opened the back terrace doors to air out the house. This would be one of the last warm days of the season before winter sneaked her silvery head in. Dimly, I heard the beeping of my answering machine and went to see who had called. Shaneika left a message that the complaint about the damaged Stephen Powell work had been reviewed. The city would pay for repair work if Stephen Powell could fix it. If that didn't pan out, I would have to sue the city for full damages and take my chances within the system.

I pushed the recorder button again. The second message was from Mr. Haggard, left only an hour ago. "Mrs. Reynolds, this is Joe Haggard. I have your casserole dish ready for you. It was good eatin'. Thanks. You might want to know that your friend, Miss Tellie, seems to be leaving on a trip. She's loading up her car. Thought you might want to say goodbye in person, you being such a close friend and all."

I grabbed my car keys, not even taking off my beesuit, and jumped into my van. Praying all the way that I might not be too late, I screeched into the Pidgeons' driveway just as Tellie was closing the back door of her Suburban. She looked up in surprise, her face clouding with anger.

"You gave me a start, Josiah," she said, trying to hide her dismay at seeing me.

I got out of my van and looked into hers. "Going somewhere?"

"Just a small trip over to Gatlinburg to calm my nerves."

"All this luggage just to go to Gatlinburg? It looks to me like you are going to be away for a long time."

"Would you please move your van? I need to get going."

"Looks like you've been in an accident," I said rubbing a dent in her fender. "Why, it seems that this car has hit a black car, maybe a black Mercedes."

"I am telling you one last time to move your piece of junk out of my way." Tellie started towards me.

I drew my taser out of my pocket. "You're not going anywhere, Tellie. We need to get some things settled."

"This is kidnapping. Aren't you in enough trouble with the police without adding this?"

"Tellie, I will not hesitate to use this on you," I warned.

In a flash, Tellie propelled herself into her car, locking the door. She then turned on the Suburban. I pulled a hive knife out of my pocket and sliced off her tire's air valve.

"You bitch!" she mouthed. *I was getting really tired of people calling me that.* She flew out of the car towards me with her hands extended as though she was going to rip off my face. I zapped her with my taser.

She fell to the ground crying and writhing.

"Tellie, that was just a little sting, but if you come at me again, I'm gonna give it to you full blast." I pulled out my cell phone from another pocket, punched in 911 and held it up for her to see; then I secretly turned on the phone's video just as Franklin had taught me.

She kept rolling and moaning on the ground as though really injured. I was not going to fall for that trick.

"Tellie, if you don't simmer down, I am going to call the police and let them talk to you. I know you killed Richard and tried to blame it on me."

She turned to look at me and my spine tingled. I had

never seen such a look of pure fury. Her face was twisted with it. Tellie rolled over and weakly stood up using the car for support.

I jabbed the taser in her direction. "Don't come any closer," I cautioned. I felt the sweat drip down my back. I was scared of her. Tellie was younger and stronger. She had to have a lot of hate in her to kill her husband. I did not want to get into a tussle with someone like that.

"You have nothing, Josiah. Let me be."

"Then let's call the cops. As you say, this is technically a kidnapping. I am sure they would like to know my theory that you jabbed Richard with adrenaline inducing his heart attack, and used the bee stings to disguise the holes in his neck."

Tellie's face slumped with the crooked look of defeat.

"What do you know?" she whispered.

"I know how and why you killed Richard. I just don't know why you picked me as the fall guy. What had I ever done to you?"

Looking defeated, Tellie leaned against her car. "It wasn't personal. It was . . . just opportunity. Richard didn't like your competition at the Farmers' Market. Said over and over again you had no business being there when he had to make a living and you being rich and all. Over time, he became more and more obsessed with you. Told people that you cut your honey with corn syrup. One day, it came to me that I could use his obsession of you to get rid of him. I never thought you would ever get convicted, even if you went to trial. Rich people never go to jail."

"Do you have any idea of what you have put me through? How much money you have cost me?"

"Josiah, it was easy to set you up. If another beekeeper had been having trouble with Richard, then I would have used him. Like I said, you were convenient."

"Meaning the argument at the State Fair."

"Yes. You and Richard were so busy eyeballin' each other that it was easy for me to switch the tags on the jars. Nobody paid any attention to me, no one ever does. And you just left the claim tickets out in the open where anyone could get at them. It didn't occur to me that he would actually push you, but when he did – so much the better for me. Then you pushed him back. He wasn't expecting that."

"Well, that certainly makes me feel better that it wasn't personal," I growled. "How did you make a call on my cell phone?"

"That was easy too. Don't you remember you sat near me at the Beekeepers' Meeting in August? When everyone was loading up their plates during the potluck, including you, I simply hung back. Your back was turned; your purse was open and the cell phone on the top. Richard had our phone turned off at the time, besides he never would have thought to check the time or date that the call was made. I told him I took the call. We had just one phone between the two of us and shared it."

"What was the purpose?"

"I had to have a record that you contacted him. Just more smoke and mirrors. I told Richard that you had called and wanted to see him. You were thinking of selling out and wanted to give him first crack at buying your bees."

"So you lured him to my house and stabbed him with adrenaline pens."

"He was overweight. Had high blood pressure. The doctor had him on medication. I didn't know if it would really work, but it was my only chance to be free. I tased him first and just pushed him in where he had pulled some frames out. The hive was already open where he was checking it. Then I stuck him in the neck with the pens in the taser burn area and started banging on the side of the hive. It didn't take much to get those bees stirred up. It was a hard thing to do, but I was desperate to get away from him. To get Taffy away from him."

"Oh come on. I think the $750,000 life insurance policy may have been the main incentive."

"An incentive – not the motive. The life insurance policy was just the icing on the cake. I had thought of a way to get rid of that wretched man for once and for all." Tellie exhaled. "You have no idea what freedom tastes like until you have been kept in a cage. I waited years for an opportunity to kill him."

"What did you have to do with the letters and the attempts on my life?"

"That was all Nancy's doing. One of the reasons I am leaving this town is to get Taffy away from that lunatic. As soon as I bail Taffy out, we're leaving Lexington forever."

"Skipping out on her court date?"

"Skip out, drop out. I don't care what you call it. I am taking my daughter and shaking the dust of this snobby town off my shoes. We are going to start fresh and clean where no one knows us."

"Taffy will be a fugitive for the rest of her life. Think about what you're doing," I said.

"My daughter will have the special tutoring and education she needs. For the first time, she will have a chance at a good life, and not just the crumbs. I'm not going to waste the insurance money on a trial lawyer when I can use it for her college education. I made a choice of what to do with the money that is left. I am going to give my daughter every advantage in the world. All my married life, I took the brunt of Richard's anger trying to protect Taffy. And I will go on protecting her until the day I die. Taffy is going to have the life I didn't."

"You're defaulting on your house?"

Tellie smirked. "The house was paid in full this morning and will go on the market in two weeks. My lawyer is handling all the details. And once the house is sold, I will have a hundred thousand plus. Meanwhile, Taffy and I will be far, far away."

"Speaking of money, how are you going to be free of Joyce?"

Tellie looked confused. "Don't know what you mean."

"Come on, isn't she blackmailing you because she covered the last half hour of your shift and lied for you so you could have an alibi?"

"Don't you dare drag Joyce into this! She's my friend. You have no idea what you are talking about."

"I know that she stupidly deposited twenty thousand dollars in her bank account, her payoff to lie for you."

"Joyce knew nothing, asked for nothing. I asked her to cover for me that day, lied to her saying that I was meeting a man. She knew about my marital problems, so she was happy for me when I told her that I had met someone special. When I got the insurance check, I gave her that money."

"As a payoff."

"No! As a gift to a friend. She wants to take her dying child to Disneyland. I gave her the twenty thousand so that she and her son could have everything their hearts desired on this trip. She knew nothing about my plans. She thinks I am leaving to meet this made-up man just for the weekend."

That certainly knocked the wind out of my sails, but I refused to let sentimentality cloud my judgment. I was fighting for something too – me. "You could have just left Richard like Agnes did."

"Left him?" Tellie was indignant. "That's what everybody says who has never been faced with a woman beater. I did leave him. See what it got me." She pulled up her sweater. There were faded scars on the inside of her arms, looking like someone had carved a face on a pumpkin. "I ran away with Taffy when she was eight. It took him over a year, but he tracked me all the way up in Seattle, where I was working as a waitress." She shook her arm at me. "This was my punishment. He told me while I was lying in my own blood, that the next time he would take it out on Taffy."

"Why didn't you go to the police, the women's shelter, something other than murder?"

Tellie laughed out loud. "What do you think would have happened when he got out on bail and that is, if he got a judge who took my situation seriously? How many women are killed each year in this country by angry, estranged husbands? Just in this city alone?"

"Too many," I agreed.

"Do you think an EPO is any protection? It's a crummy piece of paper. Unless a battered woman has the money to hire a bodyguard, she's a sitting duck. You know it.

"The law is no use to women like me. The law doesn't protect women like me. It's all in the man's favor. And don't quote me the law, Josiah. The law states that I can only defend myself while I am being attacked. Why should I wait until I am the most vulnerable? Even at Richard's weakest, he was stronger than me. He liked to sucker punch. Most of the time, the blows came so fast I didn't have time to move out of the way. You can call the police but I don't deserve to go to jail. I don't deserve one hour of punishment. Richard got what was coming to him."

Her tired bloodshot eyes pleaded with me. "With this money, we can have a new start. I can live without fear. It is up to you, Josiah. Let me go. Please."

"You murdered a man! You tried to frame me for his death. Don't you have any remorse?" I cried.

"It was the only way out. You know that if I left him, he would have come for me. You know there would have been more violence. Every time he went into a rage, I would think – he's going to kill me today. I lived with death every day, then I decided I had to get him first before I tried to leave him again. I just didn't want to take a chance on it being me that was dead." Tellie pleaded, "Please. Let me live my life in peace and take care of my daughter. You know what it is like to love a child, wanting only the best for your baby. What will happen to Taffy if I am not around to guide her? You saw how that crazy nurse talked her into the stupidest things."

"Shut up," I demanded. "Don't say that. What you did was wrong."

But was it justifiable? The problem was I do believe in justice . . . but sometimes justice doesn't come from a courtroom.

*

Shaneika called me later that afternoon, saying she wanted to come over. I gave her the new gate code, as I changed it every few days. It wasn't long before her car pulled up. I was out by the pool drinking sweet tea spiked with lots of vodka and chewing on a cigar. Miles Davis' *Kind Of Blue* was playing. His was the best music to get drunk by.

She plopped heavily into a lounge chair and poured herself a drink. "Wheee, that is strong!" Shaneika exclaimed.

I pulled a wet towel from my eyes. "Has anyone ever told you that you are a very loud person?"

"Is that Coltrane playing?"

"Davis. Shhhh. You're destroying the mood."

"Why do you smoke those filthy cigars when you have asthma?"

"Self destructive, I suppose." I took a long pull.

"I guess that's better than chewing tobacco. Whose Prius is outside?"

"Mine."

"Yours?"

"A friend gave it to me."

"That is highly unlikely. You don't have any friends."

"Funny."

"It couldn't have been the check for the Mercedes. I know for a fact that check was only around six thousand dollars."

"I told you a friend gave it to me."

"Hmmm, okay, let's leave it at that." Shaneika took another sip. "Are you sober enough to talk business?"

"Just barely."

"I've got a buyer for those ten acres."

I sat up in my chair. "So soon?"

"Yep, but the price is too high."

192

"Non-negotiable, like I said."

"Won't come down on the price?"

"Nope."

"That could pose a problem."

"Tell them to take it or leave it. Who is it?"

"Me."

"You?"

"Yeah, me. Got a problem with that?"

"Ya gwonna bwuild a house?" My words were starting to slur.

"I'm going to buy a racehorse. That is my dream. My passion. I never told you that my grandfather worked for Calumet Farm years ago. He used to help train all those great champions. He'd take me to work with him, let me feed those horses, brush them. Now I am going have one of my own."

"Ten acres ain't gonna to do it."

"That is why you are going to let my horse graze on the rest of your property for free."

"Now wait . . . a min . . . ute." I struggled to find words to express my indignation. My tongue felt like a big fish flopping in my mouth.

"Look, you've got llamas, worn out horses and weird-looking sheep running around. My horse needs the extra pastureland and isn't going to bother one of your little pets."

My mind cleared a little. "I was thinking of the liability. I don't want to be responsible if your horse stumbles in a gopher hole."

"I have taken care of all that in a little document which you are going to sign."

"I don't know."

"I can't afford a big outfit. Horse farms that come on the market are way out of my reach, but you have all this land here. I'll buy ten acres. I will replace those rundown fences but you have to let me use some of your land for free and also that rickety old barn. I need a place to put all my tack and equipment. This is a win-win situation. You are land rich but cash poor. I am cash rich but land poor. We are going to do some horse trading – that's all."

I winced at the pun.

Shaneika's eyes became two large moons with twin hazel lakes. "Look, I will make you so liability free that no one can take a penny from you even if they squeezed your big titties."

"The land is raw. How are you going to train a Thoroughbred here with no track, no nothing?"

She threw the document on the table. "Aren't you tired of being a victim, wallowing in poverty like it's a badge of honor? Want to play beekeeper? Fine, but don't act like you are poor when you have all of this." She waved at the house. "Sell some paintings. Buy some new clothes, get your hair done and get on with it. You're not the only woman to have her heart broken by some man."

I *was* tired of being poor. I *was* tired of wallowing in self-pity. If Tellie had the courage to make a new life, so did I. "I'll sign tomorrow after I read it. I don't want to do it drunk. And I want a percentage of any purses."

"The only way you are going to get a piece of the action is if you help pay the bills for my horses."

"Horses! How did we get from one horse to several." I shook my head. "You are using my pastures for free, using my water, which is free, and having 24/7 guards when you are not here. Matt plans to live permanently in the cabana, and I will be here most of the time."

"Okay, two percent of the purse plus tickets to the owner's box."

"I also want to go to the horsey-set parties."

"Done. Your haggling is wearin' me out. I know that you are going to have Matt go over the contract like a fly on an overripe melon, but it's a fair deal and helps us both get what we want. The check is attached to the title. Sign it and cash the check. Easy money."

I sat back in my chair and thought about the high price of this so-called easy money. "Will you get a quilt square for the barn?"

"Yes, if that will make you cash that check. I will take care of it."

"I want something pretty and in soft colors, maybe a pinwheel square."

"I've got something else to talk to you about," said Shaneika, ignoring my rambling.

"Yeah?"

"I got an official copy of Richard's death certificate – not just a duplicate."

I didn't react.

"Also, as soon as the body was released, Tellie had it cremated. No one knows where she put the ashes. It is over for good."

Again, I didn't respond.

"And Tellie and Taffy have left town." Shaneika examined me closely.

"They have? Maybe they've gone on vacation."

"Tellie resigned from her job. The phone, the water and electricity have been turned off. They've left no forwarding address. They are gone. Looks like maybe you might have been right about them. Do you want me to pursue this?"

"Nope. Leave it be."

"It looks like Taffy is going to miss her court date."

"I don't care anymore. In fact, I dropped the charges against Taffy this afternoon. Just make sure that a restraining order is in place on both her and Nancy forever."

"No can do. You can only take out an EPO if you are a domestic couple."

"Don't we have any stalking laws?"

"Inadequate."

I just shook my head in disbelief while pulling a paper out of my pocket. "Make a copy of this, send it to me, but put the original in your safe." I was hoping that the prepaid Visa cards that I made Tellie purchase for me wouldn't spill out of my bra.

Shaneika quickly read the handwritten document. She looked at me in amazement. "This gives you ownership of all Richard's equipment and his bees – signed by Tellie today. Plus she also gave you the ownership papers to her new Prius. You want to tell me about this?"

"Nope."

"You already knew they were leaving town."

"No reason the bees should suffer. This weekend, Matt and I will go get them and bring them here. On your way out, there is a CD on the dining room table. Put that in your safe as well. Don't listen to it."

"What was said and who said it?"

Faking sleep, I began snoring softly.

"Well, it looks like crime does pay if you can blackmail," said Shaneika. "Knowing you is going to be interesting, Josiah. Don't bother showing me out, even though I know you are not asleep. I also expect a key to this house. I don't want to be piddling in the fields like some poor migrant worker."

*

Around midnight, my daughter called. "Are you going to sell to Shaneika?"

"Hello to you too."

"Well?"

"I need the money. The house needs some serious maintenance. I will pay you back too."

"I didn't pay Miss Todd one red cent. She owed me."

"That's what she said when we first met. Want to tell me why?"

My daughter chuckled softly. I took that as a no. "I guess things are looking up all the way around. The case has been closed," she said.

"With minimal damage to us both. And I've got some good news. I got a part-time teaching gig at Transylvania in the art department and I am going to sell the Stephen Powell and others from my collection."

"But you love your art collection."

"It's gotta go. I am tired of being broke; besides, there are new hip young artists in town I can buy on the cheap. Plus the house will be on tour twice a month. The bees, the teaching and the touring will get me back on my feet financially. I hate being poor."

"Looks like you are coming out of your funk."

"Three years is long enough for a hissy fit while watching the farm fall apart. These bees are keeping me broke."

"But you love them."

I sighed. "Yes, I do love my honeybees. They are magical creatures in an ugly world."

"You can't ever tell me the truth about Mr. Pidgeon's death. Ever. It would make me an accessory after the fact."

"You are assuming it was murder. I have changed my mind about that, and the death certificate says otherwise."

"I trust your instincts, that's all."

"Daughter, Susan B. Anthony once said that woman must not depend on the protection of man but be taught to protect herself."

"I doubt she meant revenge killing and I'm not going to get into a debate with you about the morality of murder," she said stiffly.

"Some men are just too mean. I think any person has the right to defend themselves. The decisions people make are not black and white but very strong shades of gray. It's hard to know what the right thing is sometimes. As my mother use to say, 'You do your best and trust in the Lord.' "

"The question remaining is – are you going to be able to live with your decision? I know something heavy went down, and you are somehow involved. All things point to it."

"Baby of mine, I'm just gonna have to find peace. God knows that I tried to do the right thing – so should you." And with that, I hung up. I hated giving her the last word. After all, we both knew deep in our hearts – there is the law, and then there is Kentucky justice.

24

That should have been the end of the trouble Richard Pidgeon caused me, but there seemed no end to his interference in my life. He was more trouble to me dead than alive.

It took several weeks in the hospital again to remember the details clearly. I do remember that the phone was ringing insistently. I had been doing repair work on some windows, taking me some time to climb down the ladder and run inside the house to the phone. Thinking the call might be from one of my two lawyers, since that was whom I talked to mostly these days, I was surprised to hear the voice of my next-door neighbor, Lady Elsmere.

"Daaarling," she said in her Tallulah Bankhead voice. "What took you so long to answer my call?"

"Working on the house," I replied between breaths. Lady Elsmere was really June Webster from Monkey's Eyebrow, Kentucky, who had the good fortune of making rich men fall in love with her and then die. Her first husband was a garage inventor, who in his spare time made some doohickey for some thingamickbob and became a multi-millionaire selling his doohickey to a big corporation. Unfortunately, he had the bad luck to die of a heart attack on vacation with June in Venice while celebrating their good fortune.

But as always, a star hung over June. While mourning the loss of her beloved husband in Rome, she ran into an elderly English lord who thought he was the reincarnation of Lord Byron. June, assuming the esteemed Lord Byron was a TV game show host, was introduced into a world of literature, art and sin to which she took like a duck to water. Noting that she was such a good companion for all his tomfoolery, the elderly lord married her and took her back to England as Lady Elsmere, where she lived for some time until he, too, died. Lord Elsmere's estate passed on to the next male in the Elsmere line, but the elderly lord left June loads of wonderful cash, just pounds and pounds of it, which she converted to the dollar when the dollar was weak. She came back to Kentucky, rich as Midas and with an English title too.

June bought the horse farm next to me several years after I had purchased my farm. Brannon refurbished her run-down antebellum house until it rivaled Tara. After her house was restored as one of the most impressive early nineteenth-century houses in the South, June got into the horse racing business. It was due to her precious Thoroughbreds that we crossed swords all the time. Her farm was a desert of grass. I was trying to let my farm revert back to nature and the seeds of my so-called weeds kept blowing on her property, thus fouling her perfect pastures. Also, my animals occasionally had the bad manners to wander onto her property.

"What is it now?" I asked sharply. I was pressed for time

and wanted to get her complaining over fast.

"I am not even going to comment on your rude tone," June commented. I rolled my eyes. "But some of your peacocks are in my driveway. You know they make a lot of noise."

"Sorry, June, I will come over and get them later today," I said, ready to hang up.

"Don't do that. I want to keep them for a while to provide ambiance."

"I don't understand."

"Josiah, you will never guess who my houseguest is this weekend."

"I give up," I said, looking at the clock on the microwave oven.

"Meriah Caldwell."

"The number one mystery writer in the country?" I was impressed.

"Yes, and I am giving a dinner party for her this Saturday."

"No, no and no. Did I say no?"

"Now don't be that way, my pet."

I shook my head. "I hate your dinner parties. They're too formal. I don't have anything to wear. I always feel like I'm dressing for a prom. Besides, I have no escort."

"I will expect you at eight in your best dress with some lipstick on. I am sending my car for you because I don't want you to show up in that wretched van of yours. As for your escort, bring the delicious Matthew Garth with you. Have you two been up to any naughtiness?"

"Matt is gay," I replied. It was time the truth about us was cleared up.

"So was my second husband, but that didn't stop us from getting married and having a wonderful time before he passed away."

I didn't respond.

"Listen, I know you hate my dinner parties, but I want you to do this as a favor to me. We go back a long way, don't we? Wasn't I one of Brannon's first clients, and didn't I help spread the word about his talents?"

"Yes, June, you were and you did." I hated it when she played the guilt card. Her contacts had helped make Brannon very successful.

"Meriah has asked to meet you, and, as you have had a suspicious death on your property, she wants to explore it."

"I can't comment on that."

"Oh, poo, of course you can. I saw in the paper that the death has been listed as a heart attack. And when have you ever followed the rules?"

"Can't you just have a barbeque and serve overcooked hotdogs in stale buns like everyone else?"

"How absurd. No one has good conversations at a barbeque trying to balance paper plates on their knees while spilling sauce down their cleavage. Dust off your diamonds, darling. I will see you Saturday at eight." And with that, she hung up the phone.

Ah shoot-fire! I could see I wasn't getting out of this one. If I didn't go, June would make my life a living hell with her constant needling complaints. I was very surprised when I asked Matt, and he readily agreed to go with me. He said he appreciated the opportunity to network. Already fishing for clients. I was sure with his good looks, Matt would soon lure June away from her present lawyer, especially if he turned on the charm. June was a sucker for the pretty boys.

After working at the Farmers' Market on Saturday, I rushed home to Franklin's waiting arms. He styled my hair in a tasteful upsweep and applied just enough makeup to hide my age somewhat, but not enough to make it look like I was hiding my age. While I was grappling with my undergarments, Franklin let the seams out in my silk black tuxedo pantsuit. There were going to be no visible panty lines for his protégé.

"The black will help to camouflage your huge butt," he remarked.

"Thanks for the confidence booster, Franklin."

Ignoring me, Franklin rifled through my jewelry box. He found diamond earrings and my pendant of yellow topaz surrounded by diamonds, some of the few pieces I had not pawned yet. He put them on and stood back appraising me. "You're not a bad-looking woman when you clean up. You have this sort of Valkyrie look going for you," Franklin said approvingly. "You're tall and you've got good bone structure. Your hair is still a fabulous red with gold streaks. It actually looks real. Do you dye it?"

"Not yet, but you and Matt are going to give me gray hairs any day."

"Well, you look as good as you're going to," he said. "Of course, while you and Matt are having a grand time drinking champagne, I will stay here like a good little hausfrau and sit with Baby."

Baby raised his massive head from my good bed sheets responding to his name. Seeing no treat was forthcoming, he rolled over on his side, taking up the entire bed with his adolescent frame and began to snore with drool seeping from his massive mandibles.

I clutched a velvet wrap around me. "Your time will come, Franklin. Just give Matt some room to work up a client list. I'll bet next year you will be making public appearances everywhere with him."

Franklin pouted. "I better be or there will be hell to pay. I am just biding my time for now."

"Thank you for your help." I leaned over to kiss his cheek. "I do look good."

"Hubba hubba," said Matt, standing in the bedroom doorway. Both Franklin and I turned catching our breath at the same time. Matt was wearing a classic white dinner jacket with a red rose in his lapel. His curly dark hair was brushed back from his forehead accenting his high cheekbones and languid dark eyes.

"Don't you look great!" I exclaimed, feeling my cheeks redden.

Matt was gentleman enough to ignore my enthusiasm. He twirled me around. "You look good too. Let's go and set this evening on fire. We'll show that Yankee mystery writer, New York has nothing on born and bred Kentuckians, for we are the descendants of Simon Kenton, Daniel Boone, Tecumseh and Jenny Wiley."

"Good lord," remarked Franklin. "I don't know who those people are except for old Daniel."

Matt flashed a smile. "Look it up on your computer, Franklin. I don't want an uneducated consort. Get to it."

We all laughed but I saw Franklin head for his laptop muttering, "I kilt a bar," as we were leaving. June's car was waiting for us at the front gate. We climbed into the old Bentley and it took us exactly seven minutes from my gravel driveway to her palatial house on a winding landscaped paved one. Matt took in the restored pre-Civil War house and gave a low whistle. "I feel like we've stepped back in history," he murmured.

"Just wait. It gets better," I replied. Before we could knock on the door, June's African-American butler opened the door. "Good evening, Charles," I said, handing him my wrap.

204

"Evening, Miss Josiah," replied Charles. Charles was wearing a white jacket similar to Matt's. I bit my lip to keep from giggling.

"This is Matthew Garth," I said introducing Matt.

"Evening, Sir."

Matt extended his arm for a handshake. Charles ignored the offered hand.

I whispered, "You don't shake hands with the help. Just nod."

Matt obeyed and nodded to Charles.

"Very good to meet you, Sir. The guests are in the library as it is a chilly evening," replied Charles.

"Thank you, Charles. I know the way."

"Very good, Ma'am."

"Will I be meeting Miss Scarlet and Mrs. Peacock in the library? I say the candlestick was the weapon," whispered Matt out of the corner of his mouth.

"Charles, is Miss June in the library?"

"I believe she is still dressing, Ma'am. Excuse me Ma'am, but I need to get the hors d'oeuvres."

I sighed heavily. I dreaded meeting the other guests without June being present and hated the way she always had to make a grand entrance. I was hungry and wanted to eat soon.

"Maybe she's got the vapors," chuckled Matt as we walked down the hallway lined with silk wallpaper and marble floors. Elegant flower arrangements from the Farmers' Market rested on antique tables in front of large hall mirrors hanging from the ceiling. Matt took in a deep breath. I knew what he smelled – the green mustiness of lots and lots of money.

"Get this," I whispered. "The butler and the kitchen help plus the farm workers are black but June's secretary and farm manager are white – just like many of the great houses before the War of Northern Aggression."

Matt shook his head in disapproval. "How does she get away with it?"

"Easy. She pays extremely well and has retirement plans for all her staff. Charles has put up with her crap for twelve years. I don't know how he does it, but I have never seen him complain or get angry with June. When Brannon and I were still together, we would have dinner over here at least once a week." I touched the walls with pride. "You know this was the first house Brannon restored. He did a great job. This house will last another hundred years without any serious repairs or refurbishing. Brannon did everything just right."

We had reached the library, which was at the back of a long corridor. I slid back one panel of the heavy pocket door into the wall frame and entered the room. Immediately the smell of dusty old books and furniture polish hit me. I was glad that I had brought my portable nebulizer along with me.

"Good evening," I said, walking towards the guests before I had the chance to identify them. I extended my hand only to find Larry Bingham sipping a brandy and staring back at me. "Larry, what the hell are you doing here?" I asked startled. "Hello Brenda," I said as an afterthought to his wife.

Larry shrugged. "I've know June for a long, long time from a case I worked years back."

"Really?"

"Yep," he replied, looking steadily at me. "I've never have had the time to accept an invitation before with my work schedule, but now that I am retired, Brenda insisted that we attend."

"I have never seen the house and wanted to," cooed Brenda, looking smug.

"I've never seen Larry in a suit and without his cap," I said. "Oh, I'm sorry. What an ass I am." I started laughing.

"That's okay. I know it is a shock, but then I've never seen you duded up either, Josiah."

"Touché."

"My name is Matthew Garth," interrupted Matt. "Just call me Matt."

"I have really forgotten my manners," I said, feeling off balance. Everyone thought Larry was a humble beekeeper, but I knew Larry used to be a star agent in the FBI. Working on sensational murder cases before he retired, his presence at a dinner party with a famous mystery writer did not bode well for me. I smelled a rat.

"And I am Reverend Humble and this is my wife, Ruth," said a tall older man, rising from his chair.

My mind flashed "as in humble pie," but I resisted saying it.

"Of course you are," laughed Matt. "I have never read an Agatha Christie story where the local vicar was not invited to the auspicious dinner party. What we need now is a thunderstorm to make the evening complete."

"I am not a vicar," corrected Reverend Humble.

"It was just a figure of speech," rejoined Matt. He turned to me and lifted an eyebrow. Matt thought people who took everything literally were impossibly boorish.

"Oh," replied Reverend Humble.

"What do you mean by 'making the evening complete'?" asked Brenda, warming to Matt.

Matt eased down beside her on a heavily brocaded couch. "Well, we have the village shaman, the constable, a knight of the law – that's me."

"No," interrupted Brenda, her eyes shining. "You are the rogue, the adventurer."

"If you like," smiled Matt. "Our hostess is a peer of the realm, her guest of honor is the detective."

"What am I?" asked Brenda.

Matt grinned at her and Mrs. Humble mischievously. "You and Miss Ruth are the beautiful court ladies that will be rescued from any sign of danger by a dashing young man."

"I like the sound of that," laughed Ruth. "I've always wanted to be rescued so I could swoon into some handsome man's arms."

"What rubbish," murmured Reverend Humble.

Larry fixed his gaze at me. "What about Josiah? What is she?"

Matt strode over to me and rested his hands on my shoulders. "Josiah is the sacrificial lamb. The innocent led to slaughter . . . that is until we catch the real murderer."

I shrugged off Matt's hands. They felt hot and heavy. "You are quite right, Mr. Humble – rubbish indeed."

"Reverend," he corrected me.

"Whatever," I replied, pouring myself a neat scotch.

"What we are missing is a doctor, someone who can tell us the manner of the victim's death," interjected Larry.

"Not necessary. Since CSI, the lay person can pretty well assess cause of death," replied Matt.

Larry scratched his ear. "I disagree, but this is your party."

"No, daaarlings, it is my party!"

We all turned to stare at a diamond-laden June tottering into the room with the aid of a cane. I stifled a laugh when I saw she was wearing a tiara. A much younger woman with streaked blond hair stood beside June wearing a simple blue chiffon gown with only a simple gold chain adorning her tanned cleavage. She was prettier that her jacket photo portrayed her.

"I see everyone has introduced themselves," commented June. I went up to June and air-kissed her on the cheek whispering in her ear, "What are you up to, you old bag?"

Lady Elsmere ignored me and introduced Meriah Caldwell to her guests. Meriah shook hands with everyone and pleasantly remarked on the weather. "I hear we are going to have a storm later tonight."

Matt choked on his drink and started coughing. Ruth patted him on the back. The rest of us grinned.

Meriah looked around. "Did I say something funny?"

"It was just before you came in that Matt was stating all that was missing was a dark and stormy night," I answered.

Meriah flashed some seriously whitened teeth. "I see. Yes, that is funny."

For several uncomfortable moments, people stared at their drinks.

At last, June interrupted the silence. "I hope ya'll goin' to be more chatty at supper. We're havin' seven courses."

"I love that accent, Lady Elsmere. Where did you acquire it?" I teased.

"Your claws are out earlier than usual, Josiah. I am from Monkey's Eyebrow, Kentucky, and proud of it. You won't find me ashamed of my humble beginnings." She nudged Matt. "I have wonderful pictures of me when I was young. I was quite the looker in my day."

"I would be pleased to see anything you wish to show me, Lady Elsmere," Matt replied with a wicked smile.

June guffawed and gave Matt a playful nudge. "Josiah, Matt is a treat. Nowadays, men don't practice the art of flirting. They are such boors."

Brenda shot a look at Larry. "See, I was right. He is the adventurer." Larry nodded in concurrence.

Suddenly, an explosion of thunder shook the room and the lights flickered. We exchanged looks and broke into laughter. Charles, stone-faced, appeared at the door and announced, "Dinner is served, Madam."

June grasped Matt's arm and proceeded out the door. The Humbles and the Binghams followed. I looked at Meriah and shrugged. "I guess I'm your escort," I said placing her hand on my arm.

"Delighted," the mystery writer replied.

Dinner was a sumptuous affair. June informed us that the menu had been borrowed from a dinner that Henry Clay had given at his home, Ashland, in honor of the French ambassador in 1849. The wine flowed, followed by champagne. I was a good little girl. I ate everything on my plate. I noticed that Meriah barely touched her food. Maybe that was the secret of how she kept so thin. She kept stealing glances at me from under her long dark eyelashes. It didn't stop me from grazing on everything in sight.

"Josiah, you seem to approve of my new cook," June acknowledged.

"June, I have rarely had a dinner so fine or companionship so . . . well . . . so companionable." I looked around. "Is that even a word?" I giggled.

"Someone has had a little too much to drink," complained the Reverend.

I wanted to retort – but kept my mouth shut – for once.

"I'm feeling a little lightheaded myself," stated Larry, coming to my rescue. "I'm like Josiah. I have eaten to the full of this most delectable food. I don't think I have ever had a better meal, even in Paris – that's France, not Kentucky. If I were in baser company, I would unbuckle my belt."

Brenda shushed him.

210

Pleased, June stood. "We will have port and dessert in the parlor. Charles, show my guests the parlor, please."

"Yes, Madam."

The guests rose as one and waddled behind Charles as he escorted us to the parlor.

Meriah brushed up against me. "Excuse me," she said. "I was wondering if I could have a word with you."

"If it is about Mr. Pidgeon's death, I can't help you."

"I know you think this is forward but I am looking for a hook for my next novel, and when June told me about what happened to you, I was fascinated. I know you have been through some exasperating trials since then, but I thought you might offer some insights."

"All I know is that I found a dead guy in one of my beehives and since then, my life has been a living hell. Look, you're the mystery writer – if you wanted to kill someone how would you have done it?"

The two of us walked into the parlor. Everyone stopped talking to listen to our conversation.

"Well, the bee stings alone could have killed anyone."

I interrupted, "Mr. Pidgeon died of a heart attack."

"Perhaps from the fear of bees."

Matt stood by the window cradling a glass of port in his hands. "Mr. Pidgeon was an experienced beekeeper and a charmer to boot. Bees never stung him."

Meriah sat down. "That's the mysterious part. Why would bees sting a charmer? Because someone made them sting him, which brought on the heart attack. It could still be murder after all."

I accepted a plate with chocolate bourbon cake. "Those are my thoughts exactly."

Reverend Humble thought for a moment. "It still could

have been something more simple. The grass was wet with dew. He could have stumbled and fallen into the hive. Your bees, not knowing him, stung him from fright and caused him to have a heart attack."

"But what was he doing there in the first place?" asked Brenda.

"That is the sixty-four thousand dollar question, my dear," replied Larry.

"What do you think, Special Agent Bingham?" asked Meriah. "Was it foul play or just an accident?"

"I'm retired now. Just plain old Larry will do." Larry looked at me. "Don't have enough evidence to decide, but I know our girl here didn't have anything to do with it."

"Why is that?" asked Meriah.

"Josiah is just too damned obvious."

"Besides," Reverend Humbled observed, "the butler always does it."

"You would be surprised at how often the employee is the killer of his employer," stated Meriah. "I have done lots of research on that subject."

"And I think in two of your books, the personal assistant is the murderer," chimed in Brenda.

Meriah bowed her head. "Thank you for reading my books."

"Do you hear that, Charles?" asked Lady Elsmere. "You might do me in yet."

For the first time that evening, Charles grinned.

While the others were discussing Richard's death, I sidled up to Larry. "What did you give Tellie at Richard's funeral?"

"I gave her a check from the Beekeepers Association."

"You told me that you left that check in her mailbox," I accused.

Larry broke into a smile. "This is why I know you didn't have anything to do with Richard's death. You asked all the right questions."

"You are not going to tell me, are you?"

"No, I'm not."

"Why?"

"Because it's none of your business," he said quietly.

I thought for a moment. "You said that Goetz and O'nan came to see you."

Larry nodded.

"I bet they shared confidences with you that they would not share with anyone else as you are retired FBI. You know, buddy-buddy stuff. I bet they told you that they suspected adrenaline poisoning had been used on Richard," I said, looking closely at Larry.

His face remained that of a poker champ but his eyes widened almost imperceptibly. "I didn't dime on you," he said evenly under his breath while scanning around the room.

"No, you didn't, but you dimed on them. You figured out what had happened from what they told you, and you warned Tellie. You came to the memorial service and handed her a note to leave town."

Larry smiled at his wife, Brenda, who glanced at him while talking to Matt. She was flushed and seemingly happy with his attention. "You're one for the cuckoo's nest."

I smiled at Brenda too. Matt was apparently ratcheting up the charm dial. "I don't think so. She knew too much about how to disappear. Even someone as smart as Tellie would need help with that." I paused. "Was Richard an FBI informant?"

Larry leaned down his face and kissed me on the cheek. "This conversation is at an end. Read something other than mysteries. It's affecting your mind."

"Kiss my big, white fanny, Larry."

He laughed. "If I wasn't in mothballs, I'd take you up on that." He walked over to his wife, who was rubbing Matt's arm much too often.

Now seated in the parlor around the fireplace, the others carried on a lively conversation about murder for almost an hour. I sat in a sulk next to Larry, who steered our conversation every which way except to the topic I wanted to talk about. After seeing Matt slip June his business card, I rose and announced our departure.

Meriah extended her hand towards mine. "It was a pleasure to meet you. I hope someday soon you will give me a tour of the famous Butterfly House."

"You're staying?"

"Yes, if June will put me up. I want to write my next book about murder in Kentucky. I shall have to be here to do extensive research," she said, looking playfully at me.

"Oh, boy," I murmured. "Matt, take me home."

Matt gave June a peck on the cheek and made our excuses. I was tipsy, I admit, but that didn't keep my mind from wondering what Larry had given Tellie at the funeral.

25

I wanted the death of Richard Pidgeon behind me and forgotten. I surely did not want a famous mystery writer poking around. This weighed heavily on my mind as Matt let me off at the front door while he parked the van. If I hadn't been half drunk I might have noticed that the front door wasn't locked. If I hadn't been immersed in Meriah Caldwell's remarks, I would have picked up sooner that something was amiss. In the distance, I heard Baby howling from somewhere in the house. That alone should have caused me to wait for Matt, but I didn't. I walked right into the living room, where Franklin was seated with his hands nicely folded in his lap with his lips tightly pursed.

"Why is Baby in the pantry?" I asked, pretty pissed off. It was then I noticed my cache of hidden tasers piled in the middle of the living room floor along with their batteries. It was only then that I turned to run when something cold and hard poked in my back.

"Too late now," said a flat, but familiar voice.

I suddenly became quite sober. "What's this all about, O'nan?"

"We're going to have a little party – you, me and this funny boy here. Are you alone?"

"Yes. Left Matt off at the cabana. I am supposed to send Franklin to him," I lied.

"Good, now I want you to sit next to your boyfriend there. Nice and easy. We are going to have a little chat."

On wobbly legs, I walked over to the couch and sat next to Franklin, who was slightly trembling – or was that me. Once seated, I ventured a look at O'nan. He was dressed in a dirty T-shirt and jeans with the knees worn out. On his feet were flip-flops. His eyes were bloodshot, and his handsome face looked dirty from beard stubble. It didn't look sexy on him. O'nan held a black Glock nine mm and carelessly scratched his face with its barrel. I knew what kind of gun it was as my daughter carried one just like it. O'nan looked edgy.

"What do you want?"

"An accounting of sorts. We are going to discuss how many times you've screwed with me."

"Let Franklin go," I demanded. "If he doesn't go show up, Matt will come looking for him."

O'nan sneered. "Good, let him come." O'nan brandished his gun. "I've got something for that queer too."

Upon hearing my voice, Baby increased his howling and scratched frantically on the pantry door.

"Can't you shut that dog up?" complained O'nan.

I stood. "Let me put Baby outside. Then you can't hear him."

O'nan grinned. "You'd like that, wouldn't you? Opening the door so you could sic that monster on me."

"No, you got it wrong," I pleaded. "Let me put Baby out so we can talk. Baby, shut up!" I yelled.

O'nan waved me back. "I'm gonna take care of this. Now you both just sit still cause I can see you from the kitchen." O'nan moved towards the pantry.

Franklin grabbed my hands looking at me wide-eyed. "What's he going to do? Where is Matt?"

Before I could answer, O'nan yelled at the pantry door. "Hey, shut up in there. Shut up, you stupid mutt!" O'nan kicked the pantry door, causing Baby to throw himself against it, trying desperately to get out.

"O'nan, your beef is with me," I yelled over the dog's antics. "Let Franklin take him out."

"Sit down. I'll take care of this O'nan style." He raised his gun.

Franklin and I shouted pleas for O'nan to stop but he fired three bullets through the pantry door. I screamed. When I stopped screaming, I realized that Franklin was crying and hugging a pillow to his stomach. He had vomited on the floor.

O'nan walked back into the living room with a cocky grin in his face.

"Why?" I asked. "That dog was locked up. He couldn't cause you any harm."

Sitting on the arm of the couch, O'nan swung a leg over my lap. "Well, you see. It's like this. You took something from me. Now I'm taking something from you. Makes us kind of even."

I wiped tears away. "What do you want?" I whispered.

"You know," O'nan said, "after that lady lawyer of yours filed a complaint against me, I was reviewed by Internal Affairs. Yes, indeed, I was. And you know what? I got demoted. I won't lose my pension. I won't lose any pay but I won't ever make primary detective again – not once something like that goes into a file." He pointed to himself. "My file." He pressed his foot into the meat of my leg. "I figure you owe me something – like a pound of flesh. You know, to make things even between us."

I winced from the pain but didn't respond. My mind was working frantically but I couldn't resolve this. How was I going to get out of this one? Had I sinned by letting Tellie go and this was my punishment? Or was this just random cosmic crap? He had Franklin and me cornered . . . but good.

"Hey, faggot!" yelled O'nan reaching across with his leg and poking Franklin with his big toe.

Franklin continued hugging his pillow and wouldn't look at O'nan.

O'nan laughed. "That's okay. I know you're scared. I would be too. Hey, Josiah, why do you hang out with nancy boys instead of real men? You got all those rich society friends, but you hang out with two queers and a really nasty black medusa. Oh, I am sorry – African American. Yeah, can't offend anyone, can we?"

I looked remorsefully at my pile of tasers. I should have done a better job of hiding them. "Maybe because they don't hold me at gunpoint in my own house and shoot my dog," I answered remorsefully.

Looking thoughtful for a moment, O'nan shook his head. "Naw, that's not it."

"You're high on something. You are not thinking straight," I said trying to reason with O'nan. "You are going to regret this. Why don't you go into my bedroom and get some sleep? When you wake up in the morning, we can talk about this some more."

O'nan brandished the gun around my head. "But that's just it, Josiah. There's not going to be a tomorrow for you. Don't you get it? Do I have to expain . . . explain, oh hell, everything to you?"

My eyes widened in fear, but I kept talking. "See, you're so high, you can't even speak correctly. Let's everyone calm down. I'll fix us all something to eat. Then you'll feel better." I rose, knocking O'nan's feet to the floor.

Furious, O'nan grabbed my hair and pushed me to the floor. I screamed while reaching up and scratching his hands. Suddenly I heard a crash and was released. I looked up. Franklin had smashed my 1952 Blenko glass vase on O'nan's head. O'nan was down for the count – or so we thought.

Franklin yanked me up, nearly pulling my arm out of its socket. We ran towards the front door but the sound of gunfire made us dive behind the kitchen buffet counter. Covering our heads, we lay splayed on the floor as a spray of bullets hailed over us. Then it was quiet. I peeked around the counter. O'nan was struggling to reload, fumbling with the clip. "Now," I cried as Franklin and I scrambled towards the front door. But we weren't fast enough.

I heard Franklin scream out in pain as he took a bullet in the shoulder. I turned my head as blood spurted in my face. I froze. Franklin slid down slowly. He was in shock. I reached for his good arm and began to drag him. Then I heard O'nan next to me.

"Tsk, tsk, Josiah," he said, gleefully pressing the gun against my temple. "If you don't stop this moment, I'll have to finish him off."

I dropped Franklin's arm instantly. It fell with a thud on the slate floor. I didn't know how many bullets O'nan had reloaded into his gun, but even one more bullet was enough.

"You're nuts," I said quietly. "Are you really going to play all the way to the end, or do you just want to torture us for a while?"

Bending over to look at an unconscious Franklin, O'nan said, "I think we have passed the playful stage, don't you? Yeah, I think it is all the way to the end." He began pacing back and forth in front of me, sometimes stumbling over Franklin's legs. O'nan had lost his flip-flops and was walking barefoot.

I got a bright idea. "Let me call Goetz. He will know what to do." I was really hoping that Matt had already called the police and they were on the way. I just had to stall O'nan.

"That putz. I hate his guts. He never said anything but I could tell he thought I was bungling the Pidgeon case. Some of the guys told me that he said that I was overly anxious to turn it into a murder case when it was just a simple heart attack." O'nan leaned into me. "But we know better, don't we, honey." He winked at me.

Suddenly the lights went out. Matt had turned off the electricity. No one knew my house better than I, so I pushed O'nan away and turned to the left, knowing that he was pounding behind me. Slamming doors, I made a beeline towards my bedroom hoping to get enough time to lock its steel door, but he was right on my heels. I could feel O'nan reaching for me. Rushing through the bedroom, I thanked God the sliding glass door was open. Bursting through the screen door, I scratched my skin to shreds. I didn't stop, though, and ran around the pool when I slipped, plunging into the water. I am not ashamed to say that I peed in my pants from fear. Bobbing to the surface, I coughed up water.

O'nan grabbed my hair again and began to dunk me in the

deep end of the pool. Panicking, I struggled to free myself from his grasp until I felt faint. When I ceased resisting, I could hear O'nan laughing manically. He pulled me out of the water by my hair.

"Sweet Lord," I prayed, "help me, please." A warm breeze played over my face and my mind calmed with acceptance. This wasn't just about me. This was about saving Franklin and Matt, who had their lives ahead of them, and perhaps Baby, if he was not dead. It was about leaving my daughter with the legacy that I went down swinging – that I fought to the bitter end.

O'nan was stronger and taller, but I had one advantage. I was forty, perhaps fifty pounds heavier than he - and I was going to use it now. O'nan pulled me up. Finding some leverage with the pool's concrete ledge, I pressed my weight down, suddenly thrusting against O'nan while digging my head and shoulder into his gut. He grunted. With all my might, I pushed against him. He lost his balance and grabbing onto me, we both fell over the precipice towards the forbidding Kentucky River. Pushing O'nan's hands away, I reached for branches of young trees growing from cracks in the palisades. I hit a ledge, knocking the breath out of me. Feeling pain rocket through my shivering body, I began gasping for air as an asthma attack started. I couldn't even call out. The pain was too much. I was starting to black out. There was only so much punishment my poor arthritic body could take. It was over. I could have used that Catholic priest now – yes, we are all here for a short time. Resigned to meet my maker, I faintly heard Matt calling and the distant sounds of sirens. And then nothing.

Epilogue

It was an hour after dawn. Mist still hung near the beehives and the grass shimmered from the dew. Matt pushed through the tall grass noting that he needed to mow the pathways to the beeyard again. Pulling his dinner jacket's collar up around his neck, he tried to keep the early morning chill from escaping down his neck. Matt's hands shook as he smoothed the dinner jacket, which was white with various stains of reddish, brown from blood and dirt. The blood was not his own but from his best friend's and his lover's. The dirt was from trying to climb down a cliff to reach a dying woman.

How could his life have unraveled in such a short span of time? Eight hours ago, he was sitting in a rich woman's parlor while sipping on smooth whisky and chatting with beautiful women. Tears formed in his eyes. After so many years of being rootless, his parents dying while still young, Matt had found a home with Josiah and love with Franklin. Was all that lost now?

Matt straightened his shoulders and faced the hives. He had a duty to perform. "Ladies, ladies, wake up," he called. He scanned the opening to the hives but saw no honeybees peeking out. It would be some hours before they would be active, but he hoped that he would be napping. Matt had to catch a few hours of sleep before he went back to the hospital.

Matt sighed. Hoping he wouldn't get stung, Matt ran around to the back of the hives and banged on their covers. He jogged fifteen feet in front of the hives. Hearing their angry buzzing, Matt smiled in spite of himself. Bending down, he could see guards and worker bees peeking out. Someone was going to pay for disturbing them at this ungodly hour. A few flew into the cool air, but feeling the chill turned back to the warmth of their hives.

"Sorry to bother you, but I've got something important to tell you," Matt called out to them. "Something terrible has happened. Josiah was attacked and is in bad shape. The doctors don't know if she is going to make it or not." Matt stopped and cleared his throat. "The reason I am telling you this is that Josiah made me promise that if anything happened to her – I was to tell you. So I am. If this is some sort of magic thing between a beekeeper and her bees, then do your hoodoo stuff. She needs it. Okay?" Matt could see that most of the bees had gone back up into the hive. "I don't want you to worry. I will be taking care of you . . . for now."

Matt rubbed his face, his skin feeling heavy from fatigue, and made his way back to the Butterfly. He hoped that the cops had finished. He would check on the house and then go to his little shack to get some sleep. Later, he would call a cleaning service to clean up the mess and blood once the house was released from investigation. He stood up on tiptoes to look down the hill at the Butterfly. He could still see a few police cars in the driveway. Goetz was outside leaning against a post smoking a cigarette. He still had his pajama top on but it was tucked into his pants like a regular shirt. Resigned that sleep was maybe still hours away, Matt stumbled down the gentle sloping Bluegrass hill towards the Butterfly. He needed to find out what was going on. Trying to climb out of his mental fog, Matt knew he needed to sit down and make a list of what needed to be done. The executive director at the Farmers' Market would need to be notified first. Then Shaneika needed to be contacted. He would make the calls when he got to the Butterfly. The cell phone in his pocket was dead.

The wind began to whip furiously. Hearing the roar of rotating blades, Matt looked up to see a black MIL MI helicopter descending into the adjoining field. The whirlybird landed with a thud. As Matt ran towards it waving, the door slid open and a tall woman in dark clothing jumped out. The woman, seemingly unconcerned with the motion behind her, waited patiently. Her tight expression was one of concern and anger.

Behind her, three men peered out from the black bird. Their severe expressions were mirrored on the shiny guns in their leather shoulder holsters. After the blades died down, the men began pulling out trunks filled with military-looking equipment. Matt saw the men put on rappelling equipment.

"The cliffs are that way. If you find him alive, bring him to me before you give him to the police. Same if dead," she barked. "I want him bad."

Matt watched the men take off for the palisades and knew there was going to be hell to pay for this fiasco, all the way down the line, starting with the police. Everyone involved was going to have a piece of his ass chewed off. Josiah's daughter had just come home.

Abigail Keam

BONUS

AN EXCITING CHAPTER FROM

DEATH BY DROWNING

PROLOGUE

He silently paddled the kayak through the chilly waters of the Kentucky River, alone except for occasional river otters slipping playfully down their muddy slides or the screech owl beckoning mournfully from a redbud tree ready to open its pink blossoms announcing spring in the Bluegrass.

There were no homes on this part of the river – just low sloping farmland on one side of the river and the high gray limestone wall of the Palisades on the other. He didn't need the lights of buildings to help navigate the river. He knew the curving green ribbon of water like his own flesh – besides, there was a full moon. He could see fine – just like the catamounts that roamed the Palisades. Ever so often he could hear one of them scream. Their eerie cries might have given a lesser man pause, but his mind was made up.

Finally he came to one of the few sand beaches on the river and beached the beat-up, green kayak, dragging it upon the loose sand. On either side of the kayak were tied red gasoline cans. He cut the ropes binding them with quick, assured movements. He tugged on a waterproof bag, checked its contents of rags, matches and lighters, and then slung it across his back. He had several miles to trek before he reached his destination. He began the march. There was no doubt or wavering in his manner. His features showed no sign of the tension that was churning in his gut.

He was not going to waste any more time thinking of an alternative. He was determined. There was a vineyard to burn.

1

Death had stood on the doorstep and knocked on my door – but I didn't answer. I didn't die. There were days I wished I had – the pain was so great.

I don't remember very much except that I awoke once only to open one swollen eye slightly to see Matt, my best friend, reading to me. Over his shoulder stood Brannon, my late husband, observing the both of us. Seeing me conscious, Brannon said, "He's reading to you from the Book of Ruth."

Ruth, my favorite story from the Old Testament, told the tale of loyalty between two women facing starvation. When the mother-in-law, Naomi, tries to turn Ruth away in order to save her, Ruth says, "Where thou goest, I go; where you lodge, I lodge; your people shall be my people; your god shall be my god; where you die, there shall I also be buried."

It was too bad Brannon had never understood this concept of loyalty when alive. Now dead, he was nothing but a pile of dust in a cardboard box stored in my walk-in closet. *What was he doing here now?* Brannon turned so I could see my daughter asleep in a chair lodged in a corner. Loyalty. I smiled. At least, I think I smiled.

Matt turned a page and kept reading. I realized that I couldn't hear Matt. I thought to myself – *why can't I hear?*

"You're deaf, Josiah," Brannon said. "From the fall." He held out his hand. "Come with me."

I'm not going anywhere with you. You abandoned me, I thought in a huff.

"Where we're going, your anger won't matter. It will be forgotten."

Go away, Brannon. Mad at you. Mad. Mad. Mad.

"Ahh, Josey, you were always stubborn," he chided, his image fading.

Closing my good eye, I slipped back into a coma. I didn't awaken until several weeks later. I couldn't stand the intense pain and would have flung myself out a window – if I could have moved. When my daughter begged the doctors to put me back into a medical coma, they refused. They were going to let me sweat it out. My daughter couldn't stand the screaming – my screaming.

I must be rotten deep inside the way I hated them, the very men and women who saved my life, but hate them I did. I loathed the way they thought they were doing me a great favor by prescribing measly dosages of pain medication. I reviled their condescension, their tired jokes and heartless procedures. That suffering is good for the soul is a fool's philosophy. I don't like pain and have no use for suffering.

Neither has my daughter. I hazily remember bits and pieces of leaving the hospital – Matt leaning over me and holding my hand, mouthing goodbye; the doctors arguing with my daughter as she had the bandages, IV's, monitors, and everything else, including me, packed up; the humming of the plane engines as I was flown to Key West where the medical profession doesn't frown on dispensing large dosages of painkillers.

I was later told the decision to move me to Key West was made on that day when I was shrieking like a lunatic about the unbearable throbbing on my left side . . . the side that impacted the cliff ledge . . . because the doctors wouldn't give me more morphine. My daughter installed me in a three-bedroom bungalow complete with a pool on the ocean. She brought in her own physician's assistant to stay with me. Then what pain medication she couldn't get legally, she bought off the black market. I didn't scream again.

During the few times I was somewhat lucid, I tried to ask her what had happened, but my lips wouldn't move.

The guttural noises spilling from my mouth were confusing and animal-like, so I fell back asleep. I dreamt I was falling, falling, falling from a cliff, plunging into the murky swirling water of the Kentucky River . . .

I sat up. Somewhere a bell rang loudly. A man with a military crew cut ran into the room and leaned towards me. He frightened me, so I tried pushing him away with my hands, but only my right hand would move and not in the direction I wanted.

Who was this man? Was it O'nan? Were we still fighting? Were we falling off the cliff together? No, that was Sherlock Holmes falling off Reichenbach Falls with Moriarty.

The strange man morphed into Basil Rathbone as he turned off a monitor. He was wearing a Key West T-shirt and shorts. A chuckle bubbled up my throat thinking of Sherlock Holmes in shorts. Sherlock turned towards the bed and smiled. There was a gap in his front teeth. Now, his face reminded me of Alfred E. Neuman's, but more exotic, more ethnic. I couldn't place why. His lips were moving and I concentrated to understand what he was saying.

Why couldn't I hear him?

"My name is Jacob Dosh. You can call me Jake. I am a physician's assistant. I'll be taking care of you," he said in loud, exaggerated tones. He held a silver pen light, which he kept flashing into my eyes. "You've had an accident, but you're all right. I need to check you. Understand? Nod yes, if that is okay." The man smiled and repeated what he had said – again and again.

It finally sank in. I nodded slightly. His hands were warm and gentle, almost caressing as they moved about my body. There were calluses on his fingers and a raised scar down the length of his left forefinger. My skin was extremely sensitive to touch.

I felt the vibrations of someone running into the room. My daughter peered anxiously from the foot of the bed and then spoke to the man. I whispered her name and tried to keep my head up, but sank back into the pillows. I mumbled, "Watson?" Sherlock and I were on a case in London.

He shook my shoulder again. "Hey, stay with us. Don't go back to sleep."

Struggling to keep my eyes open, I attempted to smile at my daughter but couldn't make my lips curl up.

"Well," said the man called Jake, checking my vital signs. "Who's Watson?"

My daughter grinned. "The sidekick to my mother's favorite beekeeper, Sherlock Holmes."

"Sherlock Holmes was a beekeeper?"

"He retired in Sussex Downs and kept bees. He wrote *The Practical Handbook of Bee Culture.*"

Jake scribbled on a chart and placed it on the end of the rented hospital bed. "I always thought Sherlock Holmes was a fictional character. I didn't know he was real."

My daughter waved to me. "Cut down on the morphine. She's ready to come back to the living."

But my daughter was wrong. I wasn't. I liked living in the dream world of Morpheus, believing I was safe,

knowing that in real time, tragedy cannot be undone.
Tragedy was a bucking horse. Sometimes you were able
to stay in the saddle and ride it out – sometimes not.
And I wasn't even prepared to put my foot in the stirrup.

Abigail Keam